Luke perched on the couch. "So. You wanted to talk."

Pacing the room, Pepper stopped to look out a window, then faced him again. Her eyes were so big in her face that she seemed startled.

"Go on," he said, "tell me what's on your mind. You're starting to worry me."

Tears jumped into her eyes, and her hands frantically wiped at her face. He didn't know what else to do, so he put an arm around her, surprised by how quickly she collapsed and put her head against his chest.

The moment was too brief. Pulling away from him, she squared her shoulders and stuck out her chin. "Luke, years ago, you and I—"

"Wait. I think I know where you're going with this. I don't even think about it much. What happened, happened. We were just kids."

Pepper swallowed hard and took a deep breath. "Well, we kids made kids."

He stared at her, p

Dear Reader,

I loved writing THE TULIPS SALOON series, and I hope you've enjoyed reading about the Forrester family. Pepper Forrester struck me as the kind of woman who held strongly to family and friends and community, and therefore she reminds me of the best of what many of my readers have shown me in their own lives. I've enjoyed the notes and letters you've sent me over the years, and thank you from the bottom of my heart for everything I've learned from you. Pepper is her own woman, but like many of you, she's strong and giving, and charms her bad boy on her terms. That, for me, is the essence of a happy ending for a heroine—my own personal happy ending is the great honor you've given me by letting me tell you my stories.

Best wishes,

Tina Leonard

Her Secret Sons
TINA LEONARD

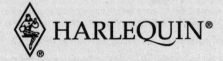

HARLEQUIN®

TORONTO • NEW YORK • LONDON
AMSTERDAM • PARIS • SYDNEY • HAMBURG
STOCKHOLM • ATHENS • TOKYO • MILAN • MADRID
PRAGUE • WARSAW • BUDAPEST • AUCKLAND

Thank you to my children, Lisa and Dean—
I'm super-proud of you!

Many thanks to Kathleen Scheibling for your support
of the Tulips series from the start!

And a huge thank-you to my readers and dear friends
who have been so loyally dedicated to my work—
your never-ending devotion has meant the world to me.

ISBN-13: 978-0-373-75157-0
ISBN-10: 0-373-75157-5

HER SECRET SONS

Tulips Saloon Red Velvet Cake

Cream 1½ cups granulated sugar and 2 eggs. Sift 2½ cups self-rising flour with ½ tsp salt. Add 1 cup buttermilk and 1½ cups vegetable oil to sugar and eggs. Slowly add flour to mixture. Mix 1 tsp baking soda and 1 tsp vinegar together and quickly pour into batter. Add 2 oz red food coloring and mix well. Makes three 8-inch cake layers.

Grease and flour cake pans. Bake at 350°F for twenty to twenty-five minutes until a toothpick inserted in the center comes out clean.

For the frosting, mix:

8 oz cream cheese (softened)
1 stick margarine
1 box powdered sugar
2 tsp vanilla

Add:

1 cup chopped nuts

Frost layers and enjoy!

—Many thanks to Julie Goode for sharing this recipe with me twenty years ago.

ABOUT THE AUTHOR

Tina Leonard loves to laugh, which is one of the many reasons she loves writing Harlequin American Romance books. In another lifetime, Tina thought she would be single and an East Coast fashion buyer forever. The unexpected happened when Tina met Tim again after many years—she hadn't seen him since they'd attended school together from first through eighth grade. They married, and now Tina keeps a close eye on her school-age children's friends! Lisa and Dean keep their mother busy with soccer, gymnastics and horseback riding. They are proud of their mom's "kissy books" and eagerly help her any way they can. Tina hopes that readers will enjoy the love of family she writes about in her books. A reviewer once wrote, "Leonard had a wonderful sense of the ridiculous," which Tina loved so much she wants it for her epitaph. Right now, however, she's focusing on her wonderful life and writing a lot more romance! You can visit her at www.tinaleonard.com.

Books by Tina Leonard

HARLEQUIN AMERICAN ROMANCE

†Cowboys by the Dozen
*The Tulips Saloon

Chapter One

"I'll be wasting my time and your breath if I
let myself care what anybody thinks about me."
—Pepper Forrester, on a warm June day to
everyone within earshot in Tulips, Texas

Men were Pepper Forrester's downfall—and her
salvation.

For the past thirteen years Pepper had lived in the
north with her aunt Jerry, bringing up her twin sons.
They were thirteen now, and they were her salvation.

She had two brothers, Zach and Duke, who were
both happy to disrupt her life, although mostly with
charm and well-meaning opinions. Her brothers
were also her salvation.

The twins' father—the man responsible for seduc-
ing Pepper out of her good sense and virginity—was
Luke McGarrett, the only man she'd ever loved. As
to why Pepper loved him, there was an obvious, yet
painful answer: he'd been glib, sexy, hot. She'd said
yes—and therefore he'd been her downfall.

But that was the past. It was time to bring closure to her life, so she'd chosen to return to Tulips, Texas, to confess the secret she'd kept all these years: she had done her own bit to increase the tiny town's population on the sly.

But while she would be proud to introduce her sons to friends and family alike, Pepper hoped that no one would suspect Luke was the father.

She comforted herself by thinking about how he had taken off after high school to find his way in the world, never to be seen again, and only heard from infrequently.

Pepper packed the last box, looking around at the place where she and the twins had lived for the past thirteen years. They'd been happy here, and yet to her, Tulips and the Triple F ranch were home, sweet home. She looked forward to the move home even though she knew her brothers were going to be mad and hurt that she'd kept their nephews from them. Duke and Zach had been adamantly opposed to their own women having a baby without them— no child of theirs would be unaware of who their father was! Unbeknownst to them, Pepper had done just that—deprived her sons of their father. She wasn't proud of it.

This would be a shock for everyone. The citizens of Tulips considered her to be an intelligent and responsible person.

Pansy Trifle and Helen Granger, town elders, members of the Tulips Saloon Gang and two of her dearest friends while she was growing up, would be stunned. Bug Carmine and Hiram Parsons, two of the local men who kept Tulips running, would have plenty of thoughts on the matter.

Pepper dreaded the confession. Thirteen years wasn't long enough for people's memories to fade. Back then Pepper had been a bright-eyed girl who'd recently lost her parents, and Luke had been her hero. She'd fallen so deeply in love that still, after all these years, she wished their relationship had been more than a high school dream.

Too bad he'd turned out to be such a rat.

Pepper had been an excellent student, determined to get into college and then medical school. Immediately following her high school graduation, after Luke had made his own departure from town—and before she really began to show—Pepper had fled to the North. Her aunt Jerry loved her in spite of everything, and helped her out with the twins while Pepper attended classes. She felt guilty for keeping the boys from their father, but knew from her brothers that Luke had never returned to Tulips, not even for a holiday. That salved her conscience somewhat.

She'd recently purchased a house in Tulips, as well as a building she'd converted into a medical clinic to service the small town. It was her way of giving back to the people who had taken such good care of her over the years; it was her way of returning with grace and honor and hope for belonging.

"Come on, boys," she said, "it's time to go home."

"I guess you're sure this is the right thing to do," Toby said.

"No. I'm not." She locked the door behind them. "But now I have my own clinic and so we're moving to where my job and your family are."

"They don't feel like family. Aunt Jerry is family," Josh said.

Duke and Zach might never forgive her for this. "Aunt Jerry may come live in Tulips next year."

"Really?" Both boys perked up.

They all piled in the car, and Pepper nodded. "I think so. After I have some time to get us settled."

"So…will our father be there?" Toby, who sat beside her in the front seat, asked.

Pepper swallowed hard. "No. He never returned to Tulips. I don't know where he is. I'm sorry."

Toby shrugged and took a last look out the window; in the backseat, Josh had his face pressed up against the glass—two sad boys saying their goodbyes to the only home they'd ever known.

"I love you both so much," she said.

"People are going to make fun of us. The kids are going to know we don't have a father," Josh stated.

"I don't think that will happen. I believe you'll be embraced with open arms. It's me everyone is going to be a little surprised by, but…" She took a deep breath…"I never said I was perfect. And you guys are my saving graces. My life is good because of you."

They accepted that in silence, and Pepper didn't begrudge them their mood. At least she didn't have to face the one thing she probably never could: Luke McGarrett. From him, she was safe.

Although after she jumped this hurdle, she really was going to have to think about introducing Luke to his sons. Somehow.

LUKE MCGARRETT HELPED three women onto the luxury yacht with his usual courteous smile. Then he assisted their father, the general, on board, as well, scanning the landscape to make certain they weren't being followed by paparazzi, mischief-makers or beggars.

It was a tough life having to guard beautiful, leggy blondes every day of his life, but someone had to do it, he thought with a grin. Being a world traveler and in the employ of the general definitely had its rewards. Mainly the scenery.

The "scenery" was untouchable, of course, since protecting them was his job, but he had to admit he wasn't attracted to the girls. If anything, he was attracted to the traveling and the money and the fact that he'd never have to return to Tulips, Texas.

He sat at the stern once everyone was seated and pulled a letter from his inside shirt pocket to reread.

Luke, you've been gone a long time. I'm getting older and need some help with the family real estate business. I'd like my only son to learn my profession and I'd like to spend some time getting to know you. I've missed that. Love, Dad

Luke put the letter away, resisting the urge to toss it into the sea. There was nothing in Tulips for him.

He didn't care about the family business. The last thing he was ever going to do was find a wife and settle down and start having kids—and he knew very well that was on his father's mind. *Oh, no, sir, not me. I'm single and proud of it.*

One of the blondes smiled at him, and he felt much better. The scenery was just so damn good it nearly hurt.

THERE WAS NO EASY WAY to do this. Pepper had thought long and hard for years about how to tell people her secret. Just imagining herself saying the words was difficult.

But it was time. So Pepper called a meeting at the Tulips Saloon, knowing it was best to tell her family and friends all at once.

Duke and Zach were seated in the antique chairs of the saloon with their wives, Liberty and Jessie, beside them, their children bouncing on their knees. Pepper turned her attention to their friends Helen Granger, Pansy Trifle, Hiram Parsons and Bug Carmine. This was her family, extended and otherwise, and the best thing to do when spilling a secret was to do it surrounded by people who loved her.

She stood, and everyone smiled at her. "Thank you for coming today and spending your Sunday afternoon with me."

There were murmurs of "That's all right" and "We're glad to have you back, Pepper." She felt tears prickling at the back of her eyes. Having left the boys in the car, instructing them to come inside the saloon in ten minutes, she wondered if she was doing the right thing. Had she ever?

"Today I'm going to tell you something I possibly should have told you long ago," she began. "I should have told you, but I couldn't." She glanced at her brothers for understanding and support. "I want to apologize to you in advance for that. A teenage miscalculation on my part, because you're the best men I've ever known…." She stopped, not knowing how to continue. They were going to be so shocked, so dumbfounded….

"Mom?" Toby said, walking through the door just ahead of his brother. "Is it time for us to come in?"

The whole room went very still. Each face was riveted upon her sons, who looked back at them shyly, their expressions holding nervousness and maybe embarrassment.

Thank you, Pepper thought. *Always my heroes, riding in to rescue me from myself.* "Yes, it's time to come in, boys." She went to hug them. Taking a deep breath, she held their hands and turned around to face the small assembly. "I'd like to introduce you all to my sons, Toby and Josh. They're my family and the reason for my being."

No one said a word. Pepper thought she saw sympathy in Liberty's and Jessie's faces, but everyone else sat thunderstruck.

Helen rose first, walking to Toby and Josh with an expression of determination and interest behind her black-rimmed glasses. "I'm Helen Granger," she told the boys, with a solemn handshake for each. "We're so glad you've come to live in Tulips."

"Oh, absolutely," Pansy Trifle said, hopping up to join her friend. "This is a wonderful place for boys to grow up. You'll really like it here."

The twins shook hands with each woman, but Duke and Zach couldn't seem to move from their chairs. So their wives got up, dragging their husbands with them.

"I'm your aunt, Liberty, and this is your uncle, Duke. He's the sheriff of Tulips," Liberty said. "You also have three small cousins."

"Uncle?" Duke repeated. "How old are you boys?"

"Thirteen," they said together.

He nodded, giving Pepper a swift glance. "I've been an uncle for thirteen years." Looking back at the twins, he shook their hands. "Guess I'm the lucky one."

"Me, too," Zach said swiftly, following behind. "I'm your uncle, Zach, and this is your aunt, Jessie, and our babies, Mattie and James."

Everyone else in the room got up to introduce themselves, but the boys were stilted and awkward with the adults. After a while, Pepper knew it was time to take them to the Triple F. "We're going home now," she said, looking at her brothers. "We're going to spend the night at the ranch until we can get our things unpacked at the house. If you don't mind, I'd like to take them there by myself for some alone time. Just about an hour." It meant a lot to her that her boys not be nervous or worried. She knew how they were feeling. If she could, she wanted to keep them from being completely overwhelmed, so that they could acquaint themselves with the Triple F slowly.

"By all means," Duke said, "it's where you all belong." He looked at his young nephews. "You'll like it at the ranch."

"Mom says she's bought a house and a clinic," Toby said. "We get our own bedroom."

Duke nodded. "You like to bunk together or separately?"

"We're used to sharing," Toby said. "One room is enough." He looked up at Duke. "Will you have enough space for us?"

"Space is something we don't have to worry about at the Triple F," Duke said. "I promise you'll be in good shape while we get your house fixed up. And anyway, the Triple F will always be your home, too. You've got two, now."

Pepper felt the tears coming again and brushed them away impatiently. "Thank you."

Zach shook his head. "No need for thanks. It's your house just as much as ours."

She hadn't been sure her brothers would still want her there. Liberty and Jessie hugged her, and the tears Pepper had been determined to hold back poured from her eyes. She reached out to hug her boys to her, fiercely proud of them, glad she'd finally brought them home.

Chapter Two

The Tulips Saloon Gang watched as Pepper left with her two sons. The silence inside the place… well, Duke thought it said a whole lot. Everyone was thinking, searching their minds, trying to recover from the shock.

Duke looked at his brother. Both of their wives were seated, silently gazing up at them, as were Pansy, Helen, Hiram and Bug. Duke shook his head, completely at a loss. "We've been too hard on her over the years," he told Zach.

Zach nodded. "I was thinking the same damn thing."

Duke shoved his hands in his pockets. "Part of me is angry as hell that she never told us. The bigger part of me knows exactly why she did it."

Zach sank into a chair and Duke did the same, though he was surprised his knees would bend. He felt more like falling over, poleaxed. "We always looked to her to be the responsible one," Zach said.

"Because she was," Duke said. "Obviously. She's

managed to do more with her life than I've done with mine."

Zach nodded. "I was still sowing oats while she was finishing up med school. I don't know how she did it with kids."

"Well, clearly Aunt Jerry was a very helpful conspirator. That must be why Pepper lived up north all those years—to be close to Aunt Jerry."

"It still couldn't have been easy." Zach looked at his brother. "I wish she'd felt that she could have come to us when she was in trouble."

Duke shrugged. "I doubt Pepper ever thought she was in trouble. I think she just took care of her business, as she always has." He glanced at Pansy and Helen and the rest of the gang. "I hope everyone will take in our new family members with open arms."

Pansy gasped. "Why, Duke Forrester, how could you suggest that we'd do anything but?"

He put up a mollifying hand. "I didn't mean that quite the way it sounded. I should have said, 'Thank you for accepting our new family members with open arms.'"

Helen sniffed. "I think Pepper Forrester has more grit in her than most women I've met in my life, and men, too." She glanced at Hiram and Bug. "There's a difference between grit and being gritty."

They nodded at the friendly teasing.

"We're gonna have to teach those young boys a thing or two about life," Bug said.

"Like how to lead a parade?" Pansy asked, since he was Tulips's unofficial parade master.

"No," Hiram said, "how to be responsible."

"You live in a jail," Helen pointed out, returning to Hiram's odd propensity to reside in the one and only jail cell in Tulips. "Though you do keep your cell quite tidy."

"Yes, but I have a room at Liberty's when I feel like it," Hiram said proudly, "and I'm willing to offer it up when you all figure out how you're going to get him home."

"Him who?" Bug asked. "All of us are here tonight, except Holt, who had an unexpected hair emergency at the salon." He looked at Bug. "I hope your wife quits trying to color her own hair soon. This is the third time she's gone green."

"*Him*—the father of Pepper's boys," Hiram said, as if no one else had the sense to think clearly.

Duke sat up straight in his chair. "Father?" he repeated, his brain in a stunned fog. "There is no father."

They all stared at him, and for a moment, Duke wondered if his shocked brain had calcified in his head. What was so obvious to them that was not obvious to him? "What?" he asked. "I don't understand."

"She didn't adopt those boys, Duke," Zach said.

"I know that, damn it!" The whole situation was making Duke grumpy. "Liberty, I think I need some tea or something, please."

She hopped up to get it, setting a tiny floral teacup in front of him. How the hell was he supposed to loosen up with that little bit of sustentation? Asking for a shot of whiskey in it would likely get him in big trouble with the ladies, so he bit his tongue and tried to unscramble his thoughts.

Liberty patted his shoulder, smiling down at him sympathetically.

"What?" he said. "What the hell am I not getting?"

"That Pepper had a love interest, and the odds of him not knowing about his boys are probably about as good as none of us knowing. Especially since most of us thought we were pretty close to Pepper, didn't we?" she asked, gently kneading Duke's shoulder.

"Well, hell, yeah." He looked at Zach. "So tell me."

"Jeez, Duke," his brother said, looking as if he'd rather be anywhere but four feet away from him. "Of course you know who the father of those kids is. You're just not thinking."

He didn't want to think. As far as he knew, Pepper had never had a boyfriend…. Light flashed behind his eyes as he thought back to the summer she was seventeen, with a terribly immature crush on—

"No," he said. "They can't be his. It has to be someone she met at college."

They all stared at him, and Duke's scalp began to crawl. "You're not saying those boys are Luke McGarrett's, are you?" he asked, horrified. "Why, they were never serious about each other! I don't think they had more than one or two dates before he left town, and I don't know if I'd even call those dates!"

Zach shrugged. "The boys are the right age."

Helen sighed. "And, unfortunately, they are the spitting image of Luke."

Pain crashed into Duke's chest. "I'll *kill* him!"

"You'll do no such thing," Helen said sternly. She stood up, glancing around the room. "Overreaction is exactly why Pepper never felt that she could come to us. Any of us. Think about the secrets we've kept over the years. Think about that damn box you guard so jealously in your cell, Hiram, which has every piece of information about this town in it. Everyone has something they've kept to themselves…. Only Pepper did it for a long time and with no one to advise her. Not from this community, anyway. She was just a girl when she left but now she's a woman. A mother. Don't dare think to harm someone she never felt needed harming."

Duke began to pace. "How could he not know? The weasel probably did know, and that's why he's never returned to Tulips."

"No." Bug shook his head. "Luke's old man says his boy is just lucky, which I found a strange comment from a man who didn't get along with his only child. But I don't think McGarrett meant it as a compliment. He said there was no luck in Tulips for Luke, so he hit the rodeo like many other hotheaded young men around here. He cowboyed, and won. Then he decided he needed more danger and worked as a rodeo clown. He was lucky, and saved the son of a retired U.S. general from a severe goring. The grateful general hired Luke to vacation with him on his party barge—McGarrett said it was a yacht, but to his mind, it was likely just a floating party—for the summer, though Luke's main focus is protecting the general's family. Being lucky, Luke invested the money he earned in the stock market and made a fortune. He then parlayed the money into commercial real estate investments, which were touched by gold. He's so fortunate that even the general's daughters now travel with him, considering him the best man they've ever known besides their father. Three months has turned into a year of work as a bodyguard, and old man McGarrett says the only reason he knows any of this is because of his connections in the military, some old chums of his who keep up with him." Bug scratched his head. "Of course, none of this was said with a fatherly gleam of pride in McGarrett's eyes. I got the distinct impression he equates 'lucky' with 'ne'er-do-well.'"

"Oh, my," Pansy said, "I do think Pepper did the right thing, after all. I'm not sure Luke would have been the steadying influence on those boys that she and her aunt Jerry clearly were."

Helen nodded. "A man is not always the solution."

Duke's brows furrowed. "Let's not take sides against a guy we haven't seen in years. He was just a boy when he left. I was a hotheaded kid once, too, and I've turned out well, given time."

Liberty smiled. "Parenting skills are a tricky business, Duke, is all Pansy and Helen are saying. Children have been known to be raised by a mother, or grandparents, or aunts, and turn out fine."

Duke looked at his wife. "I'll just be happy that the boys are where they belong now."

"And yet," Zach said, "it might not hurt Luke McGarrett to learn just *how* lucky he really has been."

Every head turned to stare at him.

"I suppose you're suggesting we tell his father he has grandchildren?" Pansy asked worriedly.

Silence reigned for a moment as the thought sank in.

"McGarrett *is* getting up in years," Hiram said reluctantly, "though he's no friend of mine."

"He's not been a friend to many folks," Bug added, "and I say it's not our place to make that decision. It's Pepper's."

Helen shifted in her chair. "Luke's never coming back."

"Oh, he will," Hiram said.

"Maybe for his father's funeral," Bug suggested.

"Oh, boy," Duke muttered. "That's not a good thought."

Zach shook his head. "Listen, we could do something radical here."

They all frowned at him. "Last time you did something radical—" Pansy began, but Helen waved at her best friend to be quiet.

"Like what?" Helen demanded, her black eyeglasses perched on the end of her nose.

Jessie whispered in her husband's ear, and Zach nodded. Helen noted the two of them had been doing a lot of whispering, which was a sure sign of a conspiracy or a brainstorm, and right now, either would be better than what they had. "Tell us," she prompted with impatience.

"Unresolved situations are never good," Zach said, "and while I am not one to advocate being involved in other folks' business, it seems that there are suddenly a lot of people in this town who could benefit from seeing Luke McGarrett in the flesh. As I say, he's luckier than he knows, so it's not like we'd be interfering in his affairs in a bad way."

Duke looked at his brother. "You're saying because his father's old, and because Luke has two young sons he doesn't know about, that we should get him home somehow?"

"Couldn't hurt," Zach said, and Jessie nodded.

"Could hurt," Hiram said, "when Pepper kicks your tail for butting in."

"There is that," Helen agreed. "Plus she'd say we were playing matchmaker or something, and that would be awful for her to believe of us, because clearly Luke McGarrett is not the man for a responsible woman like Pepper. Lucky, indeed." She gave a righteous sniff.

Bug sat up straight. "That's exactly the way his father says 'lucky' when he's talking about Luke."

"How the hell would we find him on a floating party barge in the middle of the big blue sea?" Duke demanded. "Even if we did all vote that this scheme was a good idea?"

"His father sends the odd message through the

general's office," Bug said helpfully, "though he never gets a reply."

"What a jacka—" Duke halted abruptly, censoring himself for the sake of the ladies and children present. Although he was sure it didn't matter what he said, because they all had the same low-down opinion of Luke at this moment. "We'd do better to send a P.I. after him so it could be done discreetly, instead of using a military office, anyway."

"There's trackers over in Union Junction," Zach said.

"Yes. They came into my bridal salon one day to help out the bride of the young cowboy who used to assist Valentine in transporting cakes," Liberty said. "Blaine was his name, and his older brother's name was either Hawk or Jellyfish—I can't remember which." She nodded. "At any rate, Valentine would know how to get hold of them. I don't think they actually work out of Union Junction."

Duke stood and grabbed his wife's hand. "We'll think about all this," he said. "I'm too much in shock to make a proper decision. I'm taking my bride home, because we have a baby who's getting restless," he said, staring down into the stroller where his son, Michael Zachariah, was just starting to wake from his nap. "Nobody do anything until we have a chance to think this through."

Helen kissed him on the cheek and hugged Liberty, as Pansy did. "The Forresters sure do know how to grow a town all by themselves," she said, her voice slightly teasing. "Remember when you insisted we had to grow the town organically?"

Zach slapped his brother on the back. "Sometimes you get what you wish for."

Everyone laughed at Duke, since he'd been against bachelor balls, parades, rodeos and every other idea the Tulips Salon gang had come up with to lure settlers to the area. He'd insisted they should grow the town the old-fashioned way.

Duke put on his hat. "Well, at least I'm an uncle again. I'm pretty excited to get to know my nephews. I have a lot of catching up to do."

The Forresters all departed, leaving the four town elders to grin at each other.

"That was a great surprise Pepper lobbed into our laps," Helen said.

Pansy giggled. "I love that girl. She's so dang independent!"

Helen nodded with satisfaction. "You just wait until big brother charges in to rescue his sister from evil Luke McGarrett's neglect of his duties. I have a feeling things will be settled around here mighty fast."

The four of them sipped tea and smiled, until Helen sat straight in her chair.

"Of course, we're all assuming Luke would come home and that Pepper would forgive us for meddling," she said, and everyone groaned.

"It's too late now." Pansy shook her head. "Pepper's big brother is a man of action, as you all know, too well. He'll drag Luke back here if he

has to, once his brain starts functioning again.
Whatever he thinks might be best for his nephews is
exactly what those boys are going to get!"

Chapter Three

Luke McGarrett sat in a deck chair on the general's yacht, anchored off an isle in Greece. The scenery, as always, was good, and he was, as usual, feeling lucky.

Except for the nagging sensation that something wasn't quite right. The general and his daughters had gone into town—or the small fishing village that passed for a town—leaving Luke to his own devices. They'd acted a bit secretive, claiming they wanted to go by themselves, insisting they didn't need a bodyguard.

This was unusual, as he was normally treated as part of the family. Maybe that's what had his senses on edge. The general had insisted that he stay behind and watch the boat, when always before he'd insisted Luke watch his girls.

His neck prickled, a telltale warning that he was being watched. He knew it. That lucky feeling of warning had dug him out of investments just before they sank, and human relationships just before they got dramatic. Now it was sending shivers along his nerves. Rising, he scanned the horizon. Nothing at sea and nothing unusual from the dock into the quiet village, where fisherman worked their trade and women shopped and chatted.

A man suddenly leaped over the side of the yacht with a fluid flash of tanned skin. "Peace, brother," he said, and Luke wondered where this American had come from. Luke reached for his gun, but the big man said, "No," just as another figure appeared by his side to take it.

"Sorry," the wiry accomplice said. "We don't do guns. They're dangerous."

Luke thought he was perhaps looking danger in the face. The accomplice had long dark hair pulled tight into a ponytail and deep, serious eyes. These two wanted something, but if they wanted him dead, it would have happened without him having a chance to take a second breath. *Damn, I'm slipping.* "What's up, fellows?"

"I'm Hawk," the wiry stranger said, "and this is my buddy, Jellyfish. We know some of your people in Union Junction and Tulips, and we've had to come a long way to meet you, my friend."

Luke raised his brows. "Friend?"

Hawk nodded. "In the loosest manner of speaking. Friend of a friend, perhaps."

Jellyfish nodded solemnly. "Of course, we're not sure yet if you're really our friend."

Luke sighed. "Okay. I'll bite. What do I have to do to be your friend?"

Hawk seated himself while Jellyfish kept a lookout. Hawk ran admiring fingers over the yacht rail as he glanced speculatively at Luke. "You need to make a trip to Tulips part of your itinerary."

"My father sent you?"

Hawk shook his head. "No. He doesn't know we're here. But it's time to return to your birthplace."

"No," Luke said, frowning. "Not a chance in hell."

Jellyfish dropped a hand to his shoulder, setting off alarms inside Luke. "It would be better if you did, friend."

Jeez. "Look. Not that it's any of your damn business, but my dad and me…we never got along. The old man pretty much thought I was a failure no matter what. Why he's crying over me now is a mystery."

"You should respect your elders," Jellyfish said, and Hawk nodded.

"Not to mention that running away doesn't solve anything." Hawk eyed Luke pointedly. "But we weren't sent by your father."

"Speaking of that, how in the hell did you find me?" Luke demanded.

"Wasn't hard," Hawk said, and Jellyfish laughed.

"Ex-military connections," he explained. "Sometimes it shaves a few weeks off a mission for us."

Bingo. No wonder the general had scrammed with his precious trio. "Just great." Luke shook his head. "So, do I even have employment anymore? Or did you tell the general what a bad guy I was just so I'd go home?"

Hawk grinned, leaning back against the rail.

"Actually, you're getting a paid leave of absence. At least until you make up your mind."

Luke frowned, annoyed that his luck had finally run out. He also wasn't thrilled with the breezy way in which his life was being decided for him. "And the general and his daughters?"

Jellyfish smiled. "We've agreed to take over here until a replacement for you can be found. The general said it shouldn't be too hard."

Luke stood. "Just great. A year of my life and I'm not that hard to replace."

Hawk shrugged. "Depends upon whose opinion you're interested in, I would imagine. Someone might think you're worth a hell of a lot. Then again, maybe not. Guess only you know that."

Jellyfish nodded. "The answer lies within."

Luke gave each man a sharp look. "What the hell is that supposed to mean?"

Jellyfish shook his head. "Would you like an escort to Tulips?"

"You mean a guard?" Luke snorted. "I think I can manage it. Thanks, pals."

They grinned, setting themselves up on the deck. "You can borrow our little bicycle there," Hawk offered. "You just ride up into town and a fishing boat can take you back to the big island to catch a plane. You can be home by this weekend. The sun is heavenly here, isn't it, buddy?"

Luke ignored that, and went to pack his things. Boiling anger rolled through him. Of all the stinking tricks his old man had to pull, sending goons after him was the worst. He would have gone home eventually…one day.

No, I wouldn't. I never want to see Tulips again, or anyone who lives there.

"Just peachy," he muttered to himself, hopping out of the boat with his few belongings and giving his new "friends" a rude gesture. They laughed, and Luke privately cursed the general for so easily giving him up.

This was not his definition of being lucky.

ONCE PEPPER HAD introduced her children to the Triple F and let them settle in for a few days, she quietly—over Duke's and Zach's protests—moved them into the small home she'd bought. Pepper wanted to make the move together, she and the boys sleeping under one roof for the first time in Tulips as a family, so they would know that she'd bought the house for them. The house was made of red brick with white shutters, of a typical ranch style, and close to the clinic. She loved it, and so far, it seemed Toby and Josh did, too. There were bedrooms for all of them—even one for Aunt Jerry, once she came to stay—room to spread out and a huge backyard.

Either Duke or Zach stopped by every day, picking up the boys to run errands with them. They had a thousand excuses for spending time with their nephews. This gave Pepper time to clean the clinic and establish her practice, but most importantly, it gave her time to think about what she'd told the boys over the years about their father.

She'd been as honest about Luke as possible, deciding that the truth always came back to haunt a person. Carefully, she told the boys—when they asked—that their father hadn't been ready for marriage, nor had she. She also admitted that she hadn't told Luke about them. One day, when the time was right, she promised, they would find him and tell him.

Toby and Josh had been all right with that, somehow understanding that she was genuinely trying to act in their best interests to the utmost of her ability. As a doctor, she'd presented the facts gently; as a mother, she'd waited anxiously for tears, recriminations, bitterness.

The boys had simply taken the information into their hearts, knowing that one day they would meet their father.

Pepper glanced around the clinic. It was freshly painted and all her diplomas and certifications had been hung. She was proud of what she had accomplished. If she could make a go of this, she hoped to bring on a pediatric specialist in the future and maybe enlarge the clinic. Tulips deserved a good medical complex. That, as much as good schools, would bring people to their town, she figured. Moreover, she wanted to be able to take care of folks who had given her so much over the years.

Maybe she'd even have a door made for her clinic just like the beautiful one that welcomed visitors to the Tulips Saloon. People liked calming, pretty things when they visited a doctor, and a matching door would be symbolic. There were a lot of connected hearts in this town, and Pepper intended to honor them.

She locked the door and headed over to Holt's salon.

"Hey," he said, looking up from a magazine. "You're right on time."

"This time," she said, sliding into the chair. "I love the clinic. The boys love the house. Thank you for helping me find them."

Holt grinned, running a hand through Pepper's tangled, auburn mop. "Let's find something gorgeous here, okay? How long has it been since you've had a complete style?"

Pepper looked at herself in the mirror, smiling at the mess Holt was examining with somewhat concealed disdain. "Long enough. I've been busy."

"Yes. Now that you're back in town, you can slow down a bit. Your hair is telling on you." He began combing out her locks, and Pepper sighed with pleasure. "If our hair is our nod to the day, I hear you may be needing a real brave new look."

She looked at him in the mirror. "Are we going to share our little gossip?"

He smiled. "Perhaps. There was a council meeting the other night after you introduced your boys."

"Oh? I'm not surprised."

"All I'm saying is be on the lookout." Holt flashed his scissors. "I can't say more than that, but I do feel that a friendly heads-up is in order."

"Could you clarify?"

He sighed. "Not really. You're a Tulipian. You

know how it works around here. Still, you've been gone long enough that you might have forgotten, so I'm just reminding you."

"Should I be worried? Is it about the boys?"

"No." Holt gave her a reassuring grin. "Not in the sense you're thinking. Everyone here is glad you brought them home. But you know that, around here, love is equated with trying to be helpful."

"Well, as long as it's well-meaning...." She wondered what to make of Holt's secretive expression.

"It always is, my dear." He smiled. "It always is."

She wasn't sure that made her feel a whole lot better.

ON A CLEAR SUNDAY EVENING, at an hour when most people should be snuggled up in their beds or in front of their televisions, Luke McGarrett returned to Tulips. He was looking for zero fanfare and no welcoming committee.

Of course, he wouldn't get one, anyway.

The taxi driver sped away, glad to get back to Dallas. Luke watched as the last vestige of up-to-date civilization left him. Feeling very much the pawn,

he glanced around, deciding not much had changed. He hadn't expected it to.

The Tulips Saloon was new. It had a pretty door, with lots of stained glass flowers worked into it. Quite inviting for a man who had come a long way and who'd dreaded every step. There was an Open sign in the window, and Luke felt as if he could use some fortification before he went to see his father, so he swung the door wide.

Four gray heads turned to stare at him, and one by one, their jaws dropped.

Not exactly an enthusiastic greeting, Luke thought. "Hi," he said, "I'm Luke McGarrett."

"We know who you are." Helen Granger—he remembered her giving him a talking-to in church when he was a boy—stood to greet him. Pansy Trifle—he remembered her telling on him to his dad about how he didn't eat his lunch in the cafeteria, preferring to play outside with the boys instead—stood, as well. "You got home quick."

He nodded. "Howdy, Mr. Parsons. Mr. Carmine."

Hiram and Bug stood in turn. They shook his hand solemnly.

"A couple of fellows happened to swing by the yacht I was on to let me know I was needed here." Luke recalled how the grapevine worked in this small town. "You wouldn't happen to know anything about that, would you?"

They shook their heads. Luke sighed to himself, realizing that starting out on the defensive was going to make him no friends. Whatever was brewing in Tulips would be revealed to him eventually. "So, I guess some coffee might be on the menu? I could use some before I go home."

Pansy went to get him a mug. Helen, Bug and Hiram just stared at him, making him more apprehensive. "It's only me," he said. "I probably haven't changed all that much."

They looked down at their own coffee mugs. Luke was struck by their closemouthed behavior. When Hiram had owned the pawn shop, he'd been active in the community, and one wouldn't have called him quiet. Bug...well, Bug was Bug, and he could be given to long bouts of quiet—he liked to take off to think, and drink, solo—until Mrs. Carmine had him brought home from the fields.

"Long time no see," Pansy finally said bravely, and then he understood that maybe their feelings were a little hurt.

"I guess so," he said with a nod. "I deserve you pointing that out."

"Maybe a Christmas card or two wouldn't have killed you," Helen complained. "Your dad didn't often seem to know much about you."

"Enough for someone to figure out how to find me," he said. "Who sent the goons after me?"

"We had nothing to do with that," Pansy said. "We don't send goons, anyway."

But they all looked away, and Luke knew he wasn't getting the straightest answer. "So, do any of you want to tell me what's on your minds?"

"No," Hiram said, "we just sit at this table most of our days and drink tea. Sometimes we go to Pansy's house and sit and sometimes we sit at Helen's. But our lives are pretty much about tea and cookies these days."

Somehow, Luke doubted that. "Thanks for the coffee, then." He stood. "It was good to see you again. I'd best go see Dad."

They stared at him.

"I suppose you'd tell me if he wasn't all right," Luke said slowly, beginning to worry.

"He's fine," Bug said. "Mostly lonely, which, I'll be the first to admit, he tends to bring upon himself. Still, he misses you."

"All right." Luke tipped his hat. "I'll head that way."

They watched him leave, and at the door, he turned to look back, again catching them staring at him.

They definitely had something on their minds they weren't sharing with him. He sighed. "How about a hint?"

"No," Helen said, "we daren't."

"All right, then." He appreciated the honesty. "I'll find out on my own."

He left, and started heading to his father's.

"Oh," Helen said, sticking her head out the door. "Would you mind dropping this batch of cookies off at the new clinic? It's a grand-opening gift, you might say."

"New clinic?"

"Yes. Off Cotton Blossom street, four blocks away. You remember. Short walk."

He looked down into her eyes, searching for clues, but she gave nothing away except the cookies, which she pressed into his hand. "Thank you," Helen said primly.

"No problem."

In fact, it gave him a reason not to hurry home.

One more delay before seeing his father wasn't necessarily a bad thing.

PEPPER LOOKED AROUND her clinic, feeling proud of it, proud of her new home and of her boys. Holt had made her hair pretty and she had a new dress Liberty had sewed for her. Tomorrow was the big day. The grand opening. The day she started giving back to Tulips.

"I'm so excited," she said to herself, glad that she had one last moment to herself to enjoy her brand-new surroundings. The boys were off with her brothers, but they'd be here tomorrow to help her celebrate.

They had so much to celebrate together.

The door swung open, and Pepper turned with a welcoming smile. But the face in the doorway was the last one she'd expected to see.

Chapter Four

Luke McGarrett looked at her, and Pepper stared at him, her heart leaping like a deer. As her worst fear materialized, her veins ran cold. "Hi," she said, not ready at all for this moment.

He looked around, just as handsome and sexy as he'd ever been. "Hi. Pepper Forrester, right?"

She took a deep breath. "Yes. Luke McGarrett, of course."

He nodded. "Here's some cookies the ladies sent over for some grand opening. Is this your place?"

"Yes."

"You're a doctor?"

He said it as if he was implying *You turned out to be more than just a bookworm?*

She put the cookies on a shelf as an excuse to break eye contact. "Yes. And you?"

"I'm just…drifting," he said slowly. "I don't think I realized that until just now."

She shook her head. "I don't understand."

He shrugged. "It doesn't matter. Well, congratulations." He looked around him again. "I'll think of something cool and witty I could have said after I'm gone."

"Why?" Pepper asked, wondering why he'd bother.

"I don't know." Luke sounded surprised. "I don't remember you being so pretty. I mean, you were always the smartest student in our class, but…you've really changed."

She thought about laughing, then about slapping him, then decided it didn't matter worth a damn. Obviously, she was one virgin he hadn't thought much of after the heat of the moment. "Goodbye, Luke."

"Yeah. Bye," he said.

He stared at her so long that he made her even more uncomfortable, and awkward enough to realize she still found him the most tantalizing male she'd ever come across. *Blasted female hormones.*

It hit her that she'd made children with this man. Shock flared inside her. The boys had been just hers for so long she'd forgotten that one day… She looked at Luke again, considering. One day she was going to have to tell this hunk, this person with whom she had nothing in common, this gorgeously unreliable specimen who claimed he was just a drifter…that he was a father and that they, together, were parents.

"Let's do lunch sometime, okay?" Luke said, and Pepper shook her head.

"I don't think so."

He hesitated. "Dinner? Coffee? For old times' sake?"

She walked behind the protective barrier of an island countertop. "There are no old times' sakes for us." *Please don't let him remember us rolling around groping each other as lusty teenagers. I want to be a bookwormish memory to him.*

"There's something about you I can't quite remember—"

"There's nothing," she told him. "Nothing at all." Pointedly, she looked at her watch. "I'm sorry. I must get home."

"Family?"

She put on a coat. "Yes."

He reached to help her, brushing her cheek in the process. Tingles ran through Pepper, making her grit her teeth. "Please," she said, turning to face him. "I like to do everything myself."

His grin was, slow and sexy. "I know what I was trying to remember about you."

She held her breath.

"Some of our classmates secretly voted you Most Likely to Be Town Spinster. I guess they were wrong."

She glared at him. "As long as you're proud of being the town drifter, I'll be proud of not being the town spinster." She steered him out the door, shut it and locked it. When he turned and stared through the window at her, clearly surprised to be shoved into the cold, Pepper put a Closed sign up, then went out the back way.

She had a lot to think about.

LUKE WENT AROUND to the back of the clinic and watched Pepper get into her car. She was prettier now than in high school, though she'd been cute then in a studious sort of way. Her features had a warm glow of maturity now, giving her an appealing femininity that was new and refreshing to his jaded eyes.

He'd been lying, of course. He well remembered the last time he'd seen Pepper Forrester. His body remembered how she'd wrapped herself around him with innocent sighs of pleasure. A man didn't forget that much passion, no matter how distant the memory might be.

He also knew she'd been lying, pretending she didn't remember what they'd been to each other. A woman who gave her virginity to a man never let go of the knowledge that it had happened, for better or for worse. He hoped her memories of that after-noon—and of him—were kind ones, and his guilty conscience and ego wondered if perhaps the reason she dismissed him now was because the memory wasn't a sterling one she'd recorded with happiness.

He hoped that wasn't the case. He'd always prided himself on making women happy.

She got into her car, a serviceable minivan, which surprised him. It was almost a matronly vehicle, far too maternal for such a sexy woman. He would have imagined her, with that hair and her peaches-and-cream complexion, in some sort of fancy roadster. She was, after all, from the wealthiest family in Tulips. A little spoiled behavior from the only female of the Forrester clan wouldn't have surprised him; the age and make of her vehicle did. The general's daughters wouldn't be caught dead driving or even riding in such a vehicle, unless it was an emergency and they had Gucci sunglasses to hide behind. He chuckled to himself. Pepper was a refreshing surprise to him.

Yet he couldn't afford to linger over pleasant memories of his boyhood. His father—the reason he'd been called home—waited for him, no doubt with dragon's breath ready to sear him. There was no putting it off any longer, so after Pepper had ridden away in her mommy-mobile, Luke turned to go.

Suddenly, a thought made him spin back around. A mommy-mobile was for a woman who had children, of course. She was married, and he hadn't even bothered to scan her finger for a ring. Not that it mattered, he decided. He wasn't the marrying kind himself.

Her van pulled up beside him as he prepared to walk back to the Tulips Saloon and try to hitch a ride off the old fogeys.

"I'm going to regret asking this," Pepper said, "but where's your car?"

"Not here. I had a taxi drop me off in town. I was stalling, to be honest," he said.

She looked regretful. "So you need a ride."

"If you're offering." He raised his brows and waited, hopeful she'd say yes.

She sighed. "This is so not a good idea."

He grinned and climbed in. "Thanks. I appreciate it." He chuckled when she rolled her eyes. "We can catch up on what has happened in the past many years of our lives."

"No, thanks."

Stiffly keeping her walls up, he noted. That was okay with him. He liked a woman who didn't throw herself at a man. "You could at least ask something about me."

"And feign interest in the answer?" She shook her head. "I'm giving a drifter a lift, nothing more."

Okay, she was starting to hurt his feelings. "I don't think I've ever met such a resistant female."

"I hardly know what to say to that. The obvious reply, too obvious, is that you haven't met many bright females. But I prefer to take the high road and tell you that I'm not resistant, I'm merely busy."

"And have a lot on your mind."

"Exactly."

God, he wanted to touch her. She'd jump right out of her straight-laced skin if he did. Luke looked out the window, his ego flattened and his enthusiasm for baiting her declining. "I guess I'll relieve you of my horse's-ass attempts at socializing for the moment, then." He leaned back, closing his eyes for a second. Truthfully, it was kind of nice to be around a woman who didn't want a thing from him.

He relaxed and made himself stare out the window so he wouldn't keep annoying a woman whose naked body, he remembered, was quite beautiful.

PEPPER TRIED TO DECIDE what had made her turn back around and pick up Luke. What drove her to dance on the fiery edge of an emotional volcano? He was every bit the dark-haired scoundrel with easy charm he'd always been; if anything, time had put a glossy veneer of sophistication on him that made him more dangerously sexy than ever. The cocktail was devastating to her heart, Pepper noted, analyzing her overrapid pulse and trembling, adrenaline-laced fingertips.

One day, I'm going to have to tell him....

She couldn't imagine pushing a confession to this suave, confident man past her lips. Luke and she were strangers to each other, even more awkward than total strangers because neither of them wanted to accidentally refer to their past affair. She doubted he'd forgotten her naive crush on him and her willing surrender. Likely, he was being the gentleman by pretending to forget that it had ever happened.

It never happened, Pepper told herself. *Toby and Josh were wonderful gifts from heaven.*

But no. Her boys were wonderful gifts from the man seated next to her. She clenched her fingers on the steering wheel. "Here you are," she said, "home again at long last." She stopped the car outside the front door of the McGarrett farmhouse. Luke had become more and more quiet with every passing mile, and she could feel his dread of the meeting between him and his father. Mr. McGarrett had never been easy on him, therefore laying the groundwork for conflict, to Pepper's mind, of a son who rebelled in all the requisite bad-boy methods.

"Thanks," Luke said, opening the van door reluctantly.

She softened for a second, knowing he wasn't looking forward to the meeting. Her fondest wish would be for her sons to never dread talking to their father…when they got to know him.

Prickles ran over her scalp. Duke and Zach had never had any reason to expect anything other than respect and love from their dad, as had she. "Good luck," she murmured.

Luke looked at her. "Yeah. Thanks."

She nodded, their gazes meeting. He hesitated, perhaps recognizing sympathy in her expression, so she broke eye contact and looked at her hands.

"I hope I see you again," Luke said softly. "I have a feeling you turned out to be a very remarkable woman."

She didn't look up. She couldn't. So he closed the door and walked away. She heard his footsteps crunching up the gravel drive, and sneaked a peek. Toby and Josh walked like their father, she realized, with that same loose, arm-swinging gait of busy alertness. While the walk was cute on her boys, it was darn sexy on a grown man, giving Pepper a flash that one day, her boys were going to turn out much like their father in the girl-magnet department.

They were thirteen, not so much younger than when she and Luke—

Not letting herself think about it, Pepper backed up the van and drove off.

LUKE WALKED INSIDE his boyhood home with reluctance. The front door was open, so he didn't need the key his father kept under the cracked flowerpot. Luke had checked to make sure it was still there, knowing that nothing would have changed despite time's certain march.

The house smelled musty, closed up, like library stacks in an unventilated basement. It was a world away from the open ocean and thrilling waters of Greece. Setting down his small bag, he headed to the den, where he knew his father would be on a Sunday evening.

His dad was parked in front of a blaring TV with a cereal bowl perched on a TV dinner tray. Luke swallowed hard, looking at the round top of a nearly bald head, all that was visible from behind the green recliner. "Dad."

His father got to his feet, finally realizing someone was in the house with him. "Luke. You're back."

They stared at each other for a tense ten seconds before the older man finally stretched out his hand. "Good to see you."

Luke nodded. "You, too." He shook the offered hand with trepidation.

"Nice of you to come home to see your old man," his father began, and Luke stiffened.

"You sent for me," he said. "I assumed it was important."

"My letter?" His father shook his head. "I didn't send for you. I merely suggested you might want to take over the family business."

"It's your business, Dad," Luke said, not wanting to jump immediately into a conflict. "Thanks, though. Residential real estate isn't my cup of tea."

By the looks of his father's home, it wasn't his cup

of tea, either. There was a lot of work needing to be done, both inside and out.

Stepping back, his father accidentally bumped the TV table. When he reached to steady it, the cereal bowl went crashing to the floor, and Luke realized that he hadn't been called home for business matters at all.

His father appeared quite feeble. A flash of despair and recognition washed over Luke as the truth hit him. His dad couldn't take care of himself as well as he used to, and most certainly could no longer care for a large acreage. *My footloose traveling days are over.* Luke saw himself locked into the finality of caretaking for a man who'd never loved him or been proud of him.

He swore to himself on the spot that if he ever had children, they were going to know he loved them every day of their lives. *Every single damn day.*

Chapter Five

"There's probably a proverb in the Bible somewhere about people who meddle," Helen said worriedly as the four of them sat around a table at the Tulips Saloon. "We may all go to Hades for our part in this."

They hadn't seen or heard anything of Luke since his return. That was not a good sign, Helen thought, but worse was that they hadn't seen Pepper or the boys. Neither had Duke or Zach graced the saloon with their presence.

"It does seem that we would have heard something from someone," Pansy said, and Hiram and Bug nodded. "Remember when we promised ourselves a long time ago, before Zach and Jessie got married, that sometimes we overhelped and made things worse? So we quit the busybody business?"

"Yes," Hiram said, "but then we sort of got roped back into it by Zach. He seemed needier than his brother somehow."

"Fibbers," Helen said impatiently. "We couldn't

bear to be left out. And now we may have meddled one time, too many. Someone get the Bible and see if we're going to hell for it."

Pansy giggled. "Too late now. I say we get out a cookbook, instead."

Hiram and Bug sat up with enthusiasm. "You girls bake and us boys'll play cards and lick the bowls."

"How can I pass up that deal?" Helen said. "It's better than waiting to hear something when we probably won't." She pulled out her special recipe box. "I've got a humdinger to try on you two unworthy guinea pigs. Red velvet cake like you've never tasted."

"Mmm," Hiram said. "You just go ahead and bake off those nerves you're having. Bug and me'll be happy to try your experiments."

Pansy sniffed. "Useless."

The door swung open with more force than usual, and Toby and Josh dashed in, followed by a more sedate Pepper.

"Now, boys," Helen began, in her most grandmotherly voice, "we try to handle that door with care. It was handmade for us specially. We don't throw it open like regular saloon doors." She hugged the boys to her.

"Yes, Ms. Helen," they said, awkwardly trying to squirm out of her embrace.

Pepper gave everyone in the room a kiss. "Good news," she said. "I hired four girls for my office."

"Local?" Pansy asked.

Pepper sat down. "Of course. I wouldn't dream of hiring anybody from outside of Tulips."

"Oh." Helen nodded. "We thought maybe you'd want professionals."

"Well, they'll be professional with some training." Pepper motioned for her boys to sit beside her. "A secretary-receptionist, a nurse's aide, an insurance clerk and an office manager."

"Wow," Pansy said, "you had this all thought out, Pepper."

She nodded. "For a long time." She gazed at her boys fondly. "I always knew we were coming home, one day."

For a moment, the room went silent. "Snag a cookie from the kitchen, boys," Pepper told her sons, laying a couple of dollars on the table.

Helen shook her head. "Put those away, Doctor," she said. "The boys aren't going to eat much. There's a table back there, kids, where you can eat and have some milk, too."

Pepper laughed. "Growing twins eat plenty. You'll be sorry you introduced them to your refrigerator."

The door swung open again, this time bringing Luke. Pepper's insides went tight, and she hoped Toby and Josh would stay in the kitchen, out of sight. She wasn't ready for her secret to be out, not just yet, not while she was still getting her footing in Tulips. No one had asked her who the boys' father was, and she appreciated people respecting her privacy.

Luke looked over the group and then at her, his face tired. "I came by for a refresher sugar binge."

"I'll get you some snacks," Helen said, hopping to her feet. "You stay right there and put your boots up. I see you're wearing boots now instead of flip-flops."

Pepper hid a smile at the teasing on Helen's part, and relief that the woman wasn't going to send Luke to the kitchen, too, as she had her sons. As nice as Luke had looked yesterday in his casual beach pants and shirt, he appeared rough-and-ready in blue jeans, boots and a dark denim shirt. *But looks are not enough. Being a father is about more than looking rugged and manly.*

"How's the clinic, Pepper?" Luke asked.

"Fine. I've hired some staff." She declined to say more. In fact, it was terribly difficult to even glance at him, though she tried to in order to not seem rude. Her stomach rumbled with nerves. Toby and Josh could roll out of that kitchen any second with their customary burst of energetic enthusiasm, and she was afraid of what might happen.

Decisions needed to be made. A plan of action was desperately required, with as much structure and order as she'd put into arranging her return to Tulips. Drat Luke for snarling the smooth ribbon of her life.

He caught her gaze and she glanced nervously away. "Still don't like me?" he asked softly.

She stared at him straight on. "It's not something I think about. I don't have plans to like or dislike you."

Nodding, he got to his feet, taking the napkinful of cookies Helen gave him when she returned. He left a five dollar bill on the table, waved goodbye to Hiram, Bug and Pansy, and departed.

"Gosh," Pansy said, "he certainly can't take teasing these days."

"Was someone teasing him?" Helen asked.

"You were," she retorted, "and Pepper, too."

"He always was a wee bit sensitive," Helen said, and Pepper tried to remember if that was true.

She jumped when the saloon door opened and Luke said, "Pepper? Can I talk to you a minute?" He closed the door.

Reluctantly, she rose. "If the boys look for me... tell them I'll be right back," she hedged, and Pansy and Helen nodded.

She walked outside.

"I swung by the clinic."

Surprised, she said, "I'm not quite open for business yet."

His gaze touched her hair, making her feel self-conscious. But everything about him made her feel a little jittery, his mere presence seeming to electrify nerves in her body she'd forgotten about.

"I hope you won't mind an official visit. A curbside consult, Doctor."

She shook her head. "Certainly not." It would not be good if something was wrong with Luke. There were young boys to consider, who hadn't yet met their father....

"My dad," Luke began, and Pepper breathed again, realizing how silly she'd been. "He hasn't been taking care of himself."

"I see." She nodded. "And you'd like me to stop by and see him."

"It's a lot to ask," Luke said, but she cut him off by putting a hand on his wrist. Somewhere inside her a spark flew, so she jerked her hand away and told herself to stick with nods and handshakes.

"I'd be happy to do it," she said simply, slipping a professional mask in place.

"It's probably nothing," Luke murmured.

"Most likely, but then a visit can't hurt." Her gaze went to the curb, where a shiny black truck was parked. "Nice vehicle."

Luke sighed. "It's Dad's. Apparently, he bought it last year, but doesn't use it. He contents himself with bumping around the fields in his tractor."

Pepper smiled. "Lucky you."

She wondered why he frowned at her.

"Luck has not a damn thing to do with it," he said, then tipped his hat to her. "We're at your convenience."

Perhaps he *was* sensitive, as Helen and Pansy claimed, and she'd missed that over the years due to her googly eyed, mushy admiration for him. "After dinner?"

He nodded and got in the truck, driving away.

"All right, Mr. Sensitive," she murmured, going back inside the saloon. The gang looked at her expectantly, too expectantly, and Pepper had a warning flash of intuition.

"Oh, no," she muttered. Pieces fell into place with sudden clarity. Her breath caught painfully. "You know, don't you?"

Every single one of them blinked at her innocently, their little mouths closed. Helen's glasses caught light from the overhead chandeliers and sconces; Pansy's spectacles flashed as she adjusted them with a quivering hand. Hiram's thin frame was too straight, and Bug's round faced looked too cherubic for a man who enjoyed an occasional bender on the back forty.

Pepper sighed. "It's none of your collective business," she said sternly, and they shook their heads to agree. "No well-meaning encroaching on my private life and no plans for matchmaking or anything else that remotely involves me."

"We wouldn't dream of it," Helen said, speaking for the group. "We have no idea what you're so upset about, Pepper, dear."

She shook her head. "I think you do. I'm positive you do. But as long as we understand that there are some secrets that must be kept private, like cisterns buried deep on family land—"

"Oh, we do," Pansy said. "Consider us the most bottomless well known to Tulips."

"I wish I thought that well *could* be bottomless, but you simply must not…" She hesitated, not wanting to admit what they already knew. "There is a time and place for everything."

"Everything to its season," Bug said. "A good farmer knows this."

"Then let's keep our seasons to ourselves," Pepper said, more sharply than she meant to. When Helen got up to hug her, it made her burst into tears.

"We love you, honey," the woman said. "We'd never do anything to hurt one of our most dear daughters. We stand by whatever decision you make for you and your boys."

Pansy came to hug her, too. "All you have to do is tell us what you need from us, and we're there."

Pepper's tears flowed freely, after all the years of keeping her secret. They came too quick for her to stop, so Mr. Parsons flopped a clean, pressed handkerchief into her hand. She used it gratefully.

"I don't want to tell him," she murmured, and felt better for admitting it. Not heroic, not brave, just better.

"Well, we're behind you, whatever you decide to do," Bug said, "so rest easy on that score."

Pepper pulled away, gathering herself together to face her boys. What were the consequences of her decisions? She worried as the twins strode into the room, wearing grins and powdered sugar on their faces.

"Excellent cookies, Ms. Pansy, Ms. Helen," Toby said, and his brother nodded.

"You'll have to bake more," Josh said. "We're going to be great customers."

Pepper smiled and wiped the last traces of mist from her eyes. "You boys are going to have upset stomachs."

"It's all right," Toby said. "We have a doctor in our house." Josh nodded.

She smiled at their pride in her and hoped they'd always feel that—especially when they found out that even doctors made errors in judgment.

AFTER DINNER THAT EVENING Pepper took the boys over to the Triple F. Duke was hanging around doing some yard work, which the boys scrambled to help him with.

"I needed an extra set of hands or two," he said, handing the boys his tools. Then he looked at his sister. "To what do I owe this good fortune of visiting nephews?"

Pepper swallowed. "I need to make a house call."

"Ah." He nodded, glancing at the boys. "One that doesn't include young fellows."

She pleaded with her eyes for him not to say any more. Duke sighed and took her by the arm, leading her a few feet away from Toby and Josh.

"Pepper, it's never been my way to butt into your private life, but eventually, you're going to have to tell the boys' father. You can't hide these two, forever."

"I know." She looked up at her brother. "I just want the boys to absorb the shock of the move and being uprooted from their friends and Aunt Jerry before I say, 'Oh, and conveniently, here is your father, whom I haven't talked much about over the years.'"

Duke nodded. "You've got a level head. You'll know when the moment is as right as it's ever going to be. But I will say that it's going to be hard no mat - ter what, so look out for the best time."

Pepper began walking to her van. "I've got to go see his father. He says he's not doing as well as he'd like."

"And there's that to consider," Duke called, "not that you don't already know it."

"I do know." She got in the van, feeling the

weight of her secrecy, and drove the five miles to the McGarrett homestead.

It was more dilapidated than she'd remembered, but then again, Duke and Zach kept the Triple F in mint condition. Hardly fair to compare, when there was no one to help Mr. McGarrett. Pepper got out of the van, and Luke walked out of the house to meet her, sending her blood pressure higher.

She really didn't see how she could ever tell him. They were miles apart in lifestyle. Those moonlit teenage nights might never have existed.

"Thanks for coming by, Doc," Luke said.

She nodded. "Where's the patient?"

He jerked his head toward the house. "Inside. He doesn't get out much."

She unlocked her gaze from Luke's dark one and went inside. "Mr. McGarrett?"

"Who the hell is it?" he called back. "Luke, someone's at the door. Tell 'em we ain't buying whatever they're selling."

She walked into the living room, which smelled like mothballs and boxed macaroni and cheese. "Hello, Mr. McGarrett. It's Pepper Forrester."

He squinted at his son. "You didn't tell me you had a lady friend."

"I...no, Dad, Pepper's our town doctor."

His father bristled. "Well, if she's come to see me, I don't need a doctor." He turned back to the uncomfortably loud television.

Luke reached to turn down the TV. "Dad, I want Pepper to take a quick look at you."

His dad wheeled his head to stare at him. "No."

"All right." Pepper looked at Luke. "Bye, Mr. McGarrett. It was good to see you again." She left the room, with Luke following.

"Aren't you going to examine him?"

"No." She halted in the foyer so she could explain her position to him. "He is the patient. As such, he has the right to accept or refuse care. You wouldn't want me to violate his understanding of his rights, and therefore make him feel more helpless than he already does, which I suspect is a big part of his problem."

Luke frowned at her. "You don't think he needs some type of medical care?"

"I'm not saying that. I'm saying that his emotional needs are important, too." She met Luke's gaze evenly. "People don't respond well to being pushed."

"Well. I'm sorry I wasted your time in coming out," he said awkwardly.

"It wasn't wasted at all. It's important to build a relationship of trust with a patient."

Luke nodded. "You're pretty smart with people, aren't you?"

"I like to think my ratio of success in relating to people is getting better. I think that's a hallmark of a great physician."

He walked alongside her as she headed to her van. "Pepper, I'm sorry for all the times I was mean to you."

She stopped to look up at him. "What are you talking about?"

He appeared to choose his words carefully. "I'm sure you know I went out with you on a dare."

Her breath froze tight in her chest. "I wasn't aware of that, no."

"Oh. Well, the past is in the past now, I hope," Luke said, running a thumb under her chin casually before jamming his hand in his jeans. "I hope you can forgive me for any time I might have hurt your feelings."

He was talking about their lovemaking, she realized, feeling a soft blush working its way over her skin. "I think it's best not to delve into memories that don't serve any purpose. How does that sound to you?"

He smiled gratefully. "It sounds like a smart physician coming up with the perfect diagnosis."

She opened her van door. "I'll be back tomorrow night to visit your father, until he decides he trusts me enough to at least let me listen to his heart and take a blood pressure reading."

"Ah, yes." Luke reached to touch the stethoscope she'd neatly concealed under her blouse. "I didn't see that before. You are a sneaky lass."

She moved away from his hand, which was perilously close to her breasts. "Years of treating patients has taught me that there are some ways to proceed that are more effective than others."

He sighed, ran a hand through his hair, then apparently opted for honesty. "It's probably odd to say this, but I wish I knew the best way to proceed with you."

She stared at him, surprised. "The existing relationship we have seems to work just fine."

"Okay." He nodded with some resignation. "That sounds pretty much like a 'no, thank you.' Trust me, I'm very good at heeding those."

"What exactly do you think I'm refusing?"

He shrugged. "Me. You. Something more than friendship."

"But why?" She looked into his eyes. "Because you're scared of being alone with your father and feel you need a friend? Because you're bored of being in Tulips, already? We're too old for those types of temporary fixes in our lives."

"No," he said softly, "I think it's just plain old attraction." He bent his head, sweeping one light, almost affectionate kiss against her lips, then turned away and strode toward the house without another look back.

Chapter Six

Pepper stared after Luke, so surprised that all she could do was reach up and touch her lips. She could still feel the imprint of his mouth against hers. Why had he kissed her?

She wished desperately that he hadn't. Getting into her van, she drove away to pick up her sons, knowing that she was going to have put distance between herself and Luke. There was no reason for him to have kissed her—and when he found out what she'd been keeping from him, he was going to…well, probably hate her. She would deserve that, unfortunately.

Kissing was out of the question. Romance—unthinkable.

No doubt he was bored, or scared of being alone with his father, but she couldn't allow herself to be his amusement. "Oh, God," she murmured. "There is no way this can turn out well."

Secrets had a way of catching up with a person; she knew that. She got of her van out at the Triple F and went inside.

Duke glanced up at her with a smile on his face. He was playing poker with the boys and Zach, or at least trying to, because her boys had their cards facing up so they could be instructed.

The smile slid off Duke's face after a second as he examined his sister. "Boys," he said, "snack break. Run in the kitchen and find the brownies Ms. Valentine sent over from Union Junction. She's testing a recipe for the Fourth of July."

Toby and Josh jumped up with a whoop and headed for the kitchen. Pepper watched them go with a smile. "They don't need a second invitation, do they?"

Duke patted the chair beside him. "Come sit down."

She didn't want to let her nerves show to her brothers. "I really meant to just run—"

"Be like your sons," Duke said. "Don't need a second invitation."

She sighed, telling herself she wouldn't mention her worries. It would do no good. "All right," she mumbled, sitting down.

"Good," Duke said. "Now tell us what's wrong."

Just like she knew he would. Her brothers had always read her so easily.

"Nothing is wrong," she said, forgiving herself for the tiny fib, but Zach shook his head.

"Your face is pale. Your fingers are trembling."

She looked at her hands in surprise.

"You might as well tell us," Duke said, "or we'll sic the gang on you. Once they start digging, it will all come out, although they do their prying with tea and lots of sugary cookies."

Pepper looked at both of her brothers. "I've left something unsaid, very possibly for too long."

Duke nodded. "Yeah. Done that myself."

She took a deep, bracing breath. "When I moved back here, I wasn't expecting Luke McGarrett to also be back here."

Duke shrugged. "Does it matter?"

"It does." Pepper closed her eyes for a second, praying for courage. "He's the boys' father."

Duke and Zach glanced at each other. Then Duke shook his head. "Pepper, we love you dearly. But you didn't have to tell us this. We'd already guessed."

She blinked. "I guess it's pretty obvious."

Zach nodded. "Yeah."

"Well," she said slowly, "I actually meant the something unsaid was that I hadn't told *him*. The guilt is beginning to undo me."

"Why are you worrying now?" Duke asked. "Not to be unkind, but you've put it off a very long time."

"Perhaps I shouldn't have," Pepper said, "though I certainly always felt that I was doing the right thing. Even now, I would say I did the best thing for everyone."

"Not me," Zach said. "I would have liked to get to know my nephews sooner. I'm having to play a lot of catch-up."

Pepper told herself she wouldn't cry, not one tear. Her brothers had the right to feel this way—she couldn't blame them for that. "Multiply how you're feeling by a thousand," she said, "and that's how Luke's going to feel when…he learns what I did."

"Well," Duke said, "he's going to be madder than a hornet, but he hasn't exactly been a pillar of the community. He's made plenty of his own mistakes."

"I made *this* mistake," Pepper said bravely. "It doesn't matter what he's done in his life. It matters what I do in mine."

Zach scratched his head. "We can help you tell him, if you're thinking it's time."

She bit her lips, pondering her brother's efforts. "I can't wait long," she said. "I was out there tonight, and his father doesn't seem very well to me, though he refused to let me even listen to his chest. I had my blood pressure cuff in the van but I didn't dare take that in." She thought long and hard about what needed to be said. Her conscience was tearing her apart. "It came to me that I've also stolen from Mr. McGarrett," she said softly, "and the worst part of it is, I think he should spend his time left on earth getting to know his grandchildren, if he wishes to."

"Oh, boy," Duke said. "You really are ladling the guilt on yourself."

"Luke kissed me tonight," she said suddenly. She hadn't meant to confess that, but her emotions were so confused that she had lost her way.

"Why?" Duke asked.

"I don't know," Pepper said truthfully, "but that's when I knew he had to be told soon."

Zach was still staring at her. "No wonder you came in upset. Stay away from him until you're ready to tell him, Pepper. I can't see any way for there to be anything between the two of you. I mean, the whole situation is all screwed up."

Duke nodded in agreement. "He's definitely going to feel cheated…and mad. I agree with Zach. Lie low until you're ready. If you need us, we'll go with you for support. Don't underestimate how difficult this is going to be."

Toby and Josh came into the room, carrying milk and brownies and napkins, which they proceeded to serve to their elders.

"You can't miss out on these," Toby said. "These are the best brownies ever."

Duke nodded, his gaze staying on Pepper. "It won't change things, but at least they are super-good brownies."

Pepper ate hers without comment. They were very good, but strangely—and unfortunately—Luke's kiss had been sweeter.

AFTER THEIR SISTER LEFT, Zach stared at Duke with a frown. "We may have started a bad thing here."

"By dragging McGarrett back? I don't care." Duke picked at some brownie crumbs on the table and shook his head. "So what? I don't mind having that on my conscience." He didn't, either. Pepper had so stunned him by not telling him that he was an uncle, he could only imagine how Luke was going to feel when her secret came to light.

"I'm surprised he made a move on her," Zach confessed. "I was struck by instant desire to go kick his ass, but I told myself we'd meddled enough."

"No ass-kicking," Duke said, "because then he'd owe us one for not making Pepper tell him."

Zach nodded. "But we stay out of her business from now on."

"True. Too many good intentions pave the road to hell." Duke felt like he was waiting on a sore to heal—and he didn't think Pepper would find the healing she craved until she cleared her conscience with Luke.

"Are you mad at her?"

Duke raised a brow. "Aren't you? I mean, you've spent time with those kids. They're awesome."

"Yeah. They are." Zach smiled.

"But I respect that she did what she had to do. I'll always wish I'd been there for her. Sure." Duke sighed. "I'm grateful she's come home to Tulips now. That eases a lot of this situation for me."

Zach drummed his fingers on the table. "I figure our job is to support her now."

"Right." Duke thought about Luke kissing his sister, and scowled. "Wonder why he did it, though? Kissed Pepper," he clarified, grimacing. "Though that's even less my business than anything else."

"Why does a man kiss a woman?" Zach said. "McGarrett's a strange fish. He does what pleases him."

Duke nodded. That was a valid assessment of the man's character. Duke just hoped Pepper didn't get hurt this time.

ALL LUKE'S LIFE he'd wanted love. Perhaps he'd never couched it in those terms to himself, but he recognized that hunger inside himself now. What he felt he hadn't received from his dad, he had never known how to give.

He stopped to ponder his feelings before walking into the den to check on his father. Meeting Pepper Forrester again after all these years had opened a door in his heart he'd never known existed.

Did he want that door opened now? Bachelorhood, traveling around the world unencumbered— those were simple joys and opportunities he enjoyed experiencing to the fullest.

The door, he decided, was probably best left tightly closed. He had nothing to offer a woman. He'd been lucky in a lot of ways in his life, but he'd never tested his luck with one woman—it seemed luckier to stay away from emotions he didn't know how to share.

He was disgruntled to discover that sentiment felt somehow less than appealing now, like an old bruised apple he no longer chose to bite from and would prefer to toss in a trash can somewhere.

"Dammit," he murmured, "I shouldn't have kissed her."

"Luke!" his dad called. "Bring me a glass of water, would you?"

He blinked, staring into the darkened room, which was lit only by the television screen. Then there was his father who wanted to claim his time, another good reason to stay far away from matters of the heart. Taking care of his dad seemed like a natural transition, yet Luke still chafed at this new responsibility in his life.

Clearly, he was not cut out for commitments of any kind. Best he handle them one at a time, he decided.

But Pepper's lips had been so incredibly soft, softer than he'd remembered. He'd been too hasty and inexperienced as a youth to appreciate the gift she'd given him.

He went to get his father a glass of water, and to get one for himself. Maybe it would cool him down.

LUKE WAS SURPRISED when Pepper showed up the next night, just as she'd said she would, to coax his father into letting her do some light medical probing. "You came," Luke said to her.

Pepper looked at him oddly. "Of course. I said I would." She brushed by him when he opened the door, her air professional, and he recognized a distinctive *back off* message.

He couldn't blame her. He'd caught both of them by surprise when he'd impulsively kissed her. She greeted his father, who seemed annoyed that he had to turn down the television to try to ward her off.

Luke smiled, thinking Pepper looked unbelievably pretty today, fresh and feminine in a knee-length white skirt and a light blue top. Her hair was up in a ponytail so her face was more accentuated, and he decided he liked that look on her, too.

He was beginning to find that he liked a lot about her. Given her annoyed demeanor toward him, liking her was going to be a problem. *Rein it in, Luke.*

*Once your father's had enough of you again—which
shouldn't take long—you're back on the floating
bathtub with the general's princesses.*

It wasn't a heroic thought, but as Pepper bent over
to place a stethoscope against her previously unwilling patient's chest, Luke decided antiheroic was the
best attitude to adopt unless he wanted a few layers
shaved off his heart.

"It's not serious," Pepper said.

"No, it's not, I promise," Luke replied, and received the full brunt of her displeased glare as she
motioned him into the foyer.

"What are you talking about?" she demanded.

"I'm sorry," he murmured. "I was a million
miles away."

"Nothing new about that," she said, her tone a bit
more icy than before. "Your father has high blood
pressure, which can be easily managed with proper
medication. Without a more thorough exam there is
little more I can tell, and my suggestion is that he see
a qualified internist in Dallas. If they feel it is war-
ranted, they could recommend a cardiologist."

Luke blinked. "I don't think my father will see a
doctor in Dallas."

She drew herself up to firmly stare into his eyes.
"He gave me his word that he would."

"Oh?" Luke crooked a brow. "And how did you
manage that?"

"I told him if he didn't work to get some of his
more garden variety medical issues resolved, bigger
ones would crop up, allowing him a lot less time to

spend with his only son, who has just returned home to be with him."

Irritation crept into Luke. "I wasn't planning on staying long."

She shook her head. "While I'm not surprised, you may wish to rethink that. He is your flesh and blood."

Luke squinted, thinking long and hard about how he should reply to that, and then decided to throw all caution to the wind. "I really don't think much about flesh and blood, to be honest."

She sucked in a breath. "Luke McGarrett, how can you say such a spiritless thing? That's your father sitting in there."

"You don't understand. It wouldn't matter. Today he says he cares. Tomorrow will be different."

"And if it isn't?" Pepper asked, her eyebrows raised.

He reached out to lay a palm gently against her cheek in a soft caress. "Trust me, I know him too well."

"You *knew* him too well. People change."

"Why do you care?" he asked, letting his hand drop to his side. "You have no dog in this fight. No pawn in the war."

"Luke," she said softly, "whatever was between you has been put away by him. He's waving a white flag. Can't you do the same?"

"Did you say you were a doctor or a psychologist?" Luke demanded, unwilling to bend.

Pepper hesitated a long time before she said, "I'm just someone who cares."

His face broke into a grin he was surprised to find he couldn't control. "I knew it. I knew there was something between us. You felt it, too."

She took a step back. "No," she said, "you're looking for an excuse. I care about all my *patients*."

He frowned. "You're playing games."

"You're misreading me." She walked outside and he followed her to her van. "I need to get to the saloon, so you'll have to excuse me. I'll bring a list of internists for your father to choose from tomorrow when I come to see *him*."

Silently, Luke watched as she drove away.

PEPPER FELT SAD after talking to Luke. She drove to the Tulips Saloon, thinking about the depth of bitterness he still held for his father. Everyone in town knew that McGarrett was a tough man with few—or no—friends, and that he'd been hard on his son. Real hard. But she felt pretty certain he hadn't taken care of himself in a long time, long enough to be doing some real damage that needed to be managed with a doctor's supervision.

She wondered if Luke would care if his father passed away. Right now, it felt as if she cared more than he did about his father's condition—and it wasn't just the doctor in her who was concerned.

Toby and Josh deserved the chance to know the only grandfather—only grandparent—they had.

Her conscience ate at her hungrily. Savagely.

She had some fault in this, too. It wasn't just Luke who made decisions based on the past.

On the sidewalk in front of the saloon stood her

friends, people who had known her all her life. They were examining the front door with interest, the door they were so proud of. Behind them, Duke's dog, Molly, waved her plumed tail, happy to be part of the crowd. They made such a whimsical, picturesque, Norman Rockwell portrait that it took Pepper's breath away. *Thank heavens I brought the boys home—they might have missed all this. These are the best people I know.*

She got out of her van and everyone turned around to greet her and hug her. Instantly, she was bathed in their warmth and approval.

Until she heard a truck engine switch off behind them. Turning, they all watched Luke get out of the vehicle and walk onto the sidewalk with a stiff nod for all of them. *Which includes me, I suppose,* Pepper thought.

"Hi, Luke," Pansy said. "Stopping in for tea?"

"No." He looked at Pepper. "I want to talk to Pepper, if you don't mind."

She frowned. "We just talked."

"I decided I needed a little more of your wisdom in my life."

"I think you're fine."

"You don't think I'm fine. You think I'm letting my father down." He looked at Pansy, Helen, Hiram and Bug and then at Pepper, again. "I deserve a chance to defend myself."

"Not to me," she said quickly. "It isn't necessary. Nor did I mean to be judgmental. I'm not in a position to be."

"Still, I'd be happier if we talked."

She didn't want to speak with him. Not now. One day, they'd have a serious talk, on a topic he couldn't possibly anticipate. "I see your father in a professional capacity, Luke. I'd prefer to keep our relationship that way."

He shook his head. "I feel a need to put your opinion of me straight. I think you believe I'm not aware of my father's feelings. I think you believe that I'm being selfish where he's concerned."

"You didn't say that, did you, Pepper?" Helen asked. "That doesn't sound like you."

Pepper certainly had no right to judge him about his actions, considering her own secret. Her dearest friends looked at her with disbelief and concern, and a war raged inside her over what she, as a doctor, knew needed to be said to Luke and what she, as a woman, wanted to say to him.

She faced him and her friends, saying softly, "I'll be wasting my time and your breath if I let myself care what anybody thinks about me. I really will, at least in this regard. Luke, what I said to you about your father's health was important. I won't discuss that here. He is my patient and deserves privacy." She looked at everyone, feeling the weight of her secret and her responsibilities. "Luke, please don't presume in the future that I'm willing to discuss anything and everything in front of other people."

She looked around at her friends, her dearest companions, and knew she'd drawn an inflexible line around herself.

But she had to right now—for Toby's and Josh's sakes. Whatever she and Luke had to say to each other for the rest of their lives should be in private—as much as she loved her friends.

She and Luke were parents together, though he didn't know it, and parents needed to keep their bond, their conversations, even their disagreements, between themselves for the sake of the children.

The moment to tell him had arrived, Pepper realized, her soul tearing in two.

It wasn't going to be easy.

Chapter Seven

Pepper's declaration about not wanting to talk made Luke realize how off base he was in being drawn to her. Why did attraction have to grip him when this woman was clearly not someone he could relate to on a simple, man-to-woman basis? She was cool, perhaps even cold and professional to a fault.

She could even turn chilly on her friends, as he'd just witnessed.

"We do need to talk, Luke," she said now, and he looked at her.

"Professionally speaking?"

She hesitated. "I would call this more of a personal conversation."

Pansy, Helen, Hiram and Bug—as well as the golden retriever—took that as a cue to melt through the door of the Tulips Saloon, leaving him on the sidewalk with Pepper. "I'm listening."

"Not here," she said. "And not now."

He began to sense a level of discomfort on her

part. She was always so cool and competent, he was surprised to see her acting uncertain. Glancing over her shoulder to make sure they were completely alone, she gave him a look he would almost call pleading.

"This isn't about my dad?"

She shook her head.

"When do you want to have this talk?" His curiosity was getting the better of him, he had to admit. "The sooner the better, I always say."

"I would have disagreed with that a week ago, but today, perhaps that philosophy is correct." She seemed to stop to collect her thoughts. "There is no easy way to tell you what I have to say."

He frowned, wondering if she was going to protest the fact that he'd kissed her. *She'd really take offense if she knew how well I remember making love to her and how much I enjoyed it.*

The memory was enough to put him in danger of an erection, which would be hellish and serve no purpose. He already felt awkward and uncomfortable enough with her; sexual desire was only going to tangle him up.

He hated feeling like an inexperienced teenager, particularly when he knew that she didn't remember those stolen moments they shared. If she ever did, she certainly didn't seem to recall them with fondness, which was even more bruising to his ego. "Just name the place and time."

He wanted to get it over with, and lock his pining

thoughts for her in a dark closet, where they deserved to stay.

"I don't know the best way to do this," she murmured, "and any way is going to be wrong."

"I can't really help you with that," Luke said. "I'm the kind of guy who just spits out whatever has to be said. Trust me, you don't need to put a lot of planning into telling me something."

She stared at him, her face very nearly white.

"Are you…all right?" he asked. "I realize you're the doctor, but you look like you're not feeling quite yourself."

"I'm not," she said quietly. "Take me for a walk."

He frowned, not wanting to be alone with her. She seemed to take offense at any little thing, and with his current luck, he'd find himself touching her in some way, guaranteed to make their friendship, or whatever, more tense. "Is a walk a good idea?"

She gave him an exasperated look. "Let's just walk, okay? Don't make this more complicated than it is. Believe me, it's already…crazy enough."

He shrugged. Whatever the lady wanted, he'd provide. "Okay." He steered her away from the eyes he knew would be peering—if not now, eventually— through the windows of the saloon, and away from the jail. Silently, they walked away from the town center and toward her clinic. That was safe, he decided. She'd feel on secure ground with her own home base advantage. Then maybe he could leave her there, knowing she was safe, and be on his way before he made some error that would scare her off for good.

He'd always been so smooth with women that he wondered when he'd lost his finesse.

"My house will be fine," she said, breaking the silence they'd been sharing not so companionably.

He didn't say anything, because it hadn't been an invitation as much as a grudging surrender, and he wasn't exactly in a lather to go inside her house with her. "It's a nice June night," he finally stated. "We could sit on the porch and talk."

She glanced up at him as she unlocked the front door. "We need privacy."

"Coming from anyone else, I might think that was—"

Her expression stopped his teasing comment. "It's not."

"I figured that." One thing about Pepper, she didn't leave him with any futile hopes for a rebirth of sexual relations between them.

Glancing around her hallway, he noted her house was clean and already decorated, as if she'd lived in it a long time. He envied her ability to set down roots as quickly as she did. "I can't remember the last time I wasn't living out of a suitcase. It's been years since I lived in Tulips last."

She gestured toward a sofa in her den, a floral-patterned affair that was pretty but not overwhelmingly feminine. Overstuffed and large, it was a couch a man could lean into and not feel claustrophobic.

Yet he did. He perched on the edge, forgoing the natural lure of the comfortable softness. "So. You wanted to talk."

Pacing the room, she stopped to look out a window, then faced him again. Her eyes were so big in her face that she seemed startled.

"Go on," he said, "tell me what's on your mind. You're starting to worry me."

Her lips worked but nothing came out.

"Pepper," he said, standing to walk over to her, "if you don't relax, I'm going to call the gang over to help you. I swear you're scaring me."

Tears jumped into her eyes, and she frantically wiped them away. He didn't know what to do, so he put an arm around her, surprised by how quickly she collapsed and leaned her head against his chest.

This was new and different—a pliable, soft Pepper. She was almost relying on his strength for a change, instead of fighting him with hers.

The moment was too brief. Pulling away from him, she squared her shoulders and stuck out her chin. "Luke, years ago, you and I—"

"Wait. I think I know where you're going with this. If you think I'm being nice to you because I'm expecting you to sleep with me, that's the last thing on my mind."

Her eyebrows rose.

"Well, not the last thing," he clarified, "but it's not something I expect. I don't even think about it much. What happened happened. We were just kids."

She swallowed hard and took a deep breath. "Well, we kids made kids."

He stared at her, perplexed.

"God, that was awkward," she said. "I'm so

sorry." Her voice came out a whisper. She put a hand on his arm as if trying to comfort him, but he realized by the tenseness of her grip that she still needed support. "I was pregnant," she said, so softly he didn't think he heard her right, and then he realized he had, and his whole world bottomed out. Rapid heart palpitations tore through his chest, tightening his breath.

"You *were* pregnant?" he asked, just to make certain he understood what she was trying to tell him. "As in, *were?*" She must have lost the baby, he realized—no wonder she was so unbending and brusque around him. She probably blamed him for not using proper protection, and he guessed his condom use hadn't been exactly foolproof.

"I was pregnant and…" Her big eyes stared at him.

"And?"

"And we have two sons."

He frowned at her. The woman was nuts. He had no sons. He could feel his head shaking, his neck turning automatically, and her hand on his arm tightened more, now trying to strengthen him.

"We have two beautiful sons," Pepper said, speaking a language he didn't understand, couldn't understand and would never be able to decipher.

"No," he said. "It can't be possible."

Her hand dropped from his arm. Slowly, she went to the fireplace, taking down a picture. Her gaze on his, she reluctantly handed it to him. In the photo, two strong, healthy boys stared up at Pepper, and they were all laughing, surrounded by snow and stark, ice-lined trees.

The boys were the spitting image of their mother. *These are not my sons. I don't know them.*

In spite of the instinctive denial, he did know them. He forced himself to admit that. He looked at Pepper, searching her eyes for answers. "Why?"

"I'm so sorry." The words were a plea. "I have no excuse for what I've done."

"You think very little of me."

Her face returned to its papery-white color.

"Where are they?"

"At the Triple F with Duke and probably Zach."

Luke resisted the urge to yell at her that he had to see with his own eyes the truth he could not take in. "I'm going," he said.

"Wait," she said, clutching his arm again, "they don't know. They don't know you're here."

He turned to her. "They know I'm their father?"

"No. I never told them anything about you."

"I'll never forgive you for that," he said.

She nodded. "I know. Let me go with you. Please! This needs to be as gentle as possible for them."

"I'm going to my truck. You can get in it, but don't say a word," Luke said, his mind still not completely believing that his life as he knew it had pretty much been a lie. He had to hear their voices, touch them, before he'd know—accept—that he'd been a father. Was a father. *Am a father.*

He strode down the street toward the saloon, where he'd left his truck. Pepper followed him anxiously. Normally, he would be a gentleman and offer to get the vehicle, return to pick her up. Too much anger flowed through him.

It was impossible to slow down, anyway. He had the overwhelming urge to race to meet his destiny.

Chapter Eight

An iron band of terror tightened Pepper's chest. She'd set in motion something that couldn't be stopped now, yet a profound sense of relief warred with her fear. Luke drove quickly toward the ranch, and the whole way Pepper didn't dare glance at him.

He parked the truck at the Triple F, and silently, they walked to the porch. She let herself in and he followed. They stood under the chandelier in the hallway for a moment, and Pepper could no longer remain quiet. "They're such good kids, Luke."

He frowned at her, his dark features forbidding.

"I want this to be as calm a meeting as possible," she said, "something they'll look back on and remember was a good thing for them. Their father coming into their lives should be a positive experience."

"Not positive enough that it should have happened years ago."

"That's a discussion for another time," she said firmly. "It doesn't involve them. That's between you and me and the past."

"And obviously the future."

She didn't understand his meaning, but was satisfied he intended to handle the situation with her sons carefully. Pepper walked into the den. Duke was showing the boys how to braid rope, and they were drinking it in with huge eyes. When her brother looked up and saw that Luke was with her, he slowly got to his feet.

"Hello, Luke," he said. "Long time no see."

Luke nodded.

Pepper sensed the tension between the two big men, and clearly, the boys did, too, for they glanced back and forth at times. After a moment, Duke said, "I best get back to Liberty and the baby," and he left. The front door closed and they heard him gun the truck engine and take off.

"Hi, Mom," Toby said, and Josh nodded, always content to follow his brother.

Pepper walked farther into the room. Luke followed. "Boys," she said, "I'd like to introduce you to someone."

They didn't like the sound of that, because their brows furrowed. Pepper realized they thought she had a boyfriend, and quickly said, "This is Luke McGarrett, an old family friend."

Luke reached out as the boys got up reluctantly to shake hands with him. "Rope tricks, huh?"

"Not tricks," Toby said. "We have to learn to make one."

Luke nodded. "I do sailors' rope knots."

"You do?" This interested the boys.

"Yeah."

"Sit down, Luke," Pepper said, and the boys moved back to their previous positions.

"I think...I think I'll head home," Luke said. "I guess you'll need a ride back to town, Pepper."

"We can stay here," she said. "We're sort of half here and half at the house right now." She didn't want to accept a ride from him—and she was surprised by how quickly he wanted to leave.

He stared at his boys for a long time as if trying to decide what to do. They had busily returned to trying to practice what Duke had taught them. Luke's gaze caught hers as he glanced at her. She saw confusion and pain in his eyes, though he clearly didn't want to share his emotions. She quickly looked away.

She nearly jumped when he touched her arm. "I brought you here. I'm taking you back."

Her insides were so tight she thought she might be ill. "Boys," she said hurriedly, "Mr. McGarrett is going to drive us home. Can you gather up your things, please?"

They did her bidding, following Luke to his truck. After everyone was buckled in he drove away.

Ten minutes later he parked in front of their house. Pepper got out and the boys did, too, walking to the porch. Luke stood by his truck, watching to see they got safely inside but not coming close enough to be invited in. Pepper thought she'd feel relief; instead, she felt more confused. As if she'd betrayed him all over again.

The boys waved goodbye politely and went inside

the house. Pepper turned to glance back at Luke—
she shouldn't have, but she couldn't help herself—
and was horrified to see him wiping away tears he
didn't want her to see.

She fled.

LUKE WENT HOME, or at least to the place he'd called
home again for the past week, his steps heavy and
his heart torn. He sank into the couch near his
father's recliner.

He was beyond noticing much of anything.

"Luke?" his dad said, and Luke acknowledged
him with a nod.

"Something wrong?"

Luke couldn't speak. His emotions were tangling
up everything vital in his body.

"Are you ill, boy?"

Slowly, he rolled his head to the side so that he
could make eye contact with his father. His dad
squinted at him, then reached to flip off the television. "You look like something bit you on the ass."

How was he going to tell his father—whom he
barely knew—that there were two more people in his
life that he didn't know at all? As much as he wanted
to doubt that Toby and Josh were his children, he'd
known the truth from the stark, frightened look on
Pepper's face. Even if he'd doubted her, their pictures
bore a startling resemblance to himself at that age.
Meeting them in person was a study in similarities—
he'd seen himself all over again. Twice.

Now he knew why he'd really been called home.

If he'd recognized the children as his at a glance, so had any other person in Tulips who'd seen them.

"Dad," he said slowly, "we have to talk."

His father scowled. "I've already taken no for an answer. I'm talking to Holt about buying out my business. He's always wheeling and dealing, anyway."

Luke looked at his dad. "This isn't about that."

"Oh?" His father cocked his head. "Can't imagine what else would have you looking like your dog ran off, except going into business with me."

Luke sighed. "Dad, I'm…a father."

His dad squinted. "A father?"

Just saying the words felt crazy. Luke couldn't figure out how he was going to bring his two worlds together. "I have twin teenaged sons."

His father stared at him, not sure what to make of his pronouncement. "Where?"

"Right here. In Tulips."

"Nope." His father leaned back in his recliner. "Son, you have no children here. I'd have seen them over the years. Believe me, I wasn't always sitting in this chair. And nobody keeps that kind of thing quiet in Tulips."

Luke shook his head. "I *do,* Dad."

His father turned to him, frowning. "Who's the mother, then?"

Luke could barely bring himself to say it. No wonder Duke had stared at him last night with such intensity. Pepper, the mother of *his* children? It was like mating a black sheep with a good unbred lamb. "Pepper Forrester," he said after a long moment.

His dad started to laugh. "That little doc that comes around trying to make me take care of myself?" He stopped laughing after a moment when Luke didn't say anything. Scratching his head, he said, "Well, hell, maybe she was trying to tell me something."

Luke looked up. "Like what?"

"Like maybe I've got something to live for now."

Maybe they both did. "Pepper would want you to take care of yourself no matter what. Once you're her patient, I think it's your will against hers."

His dad arched a brow. "You like that girl?"

Luke sighed. "I'm too mad, too shocked, to even think about that."

His dad shrugged, leaning back again. "If what you say is true, you might consider it."

Luke looked up. "Why? What do you mean?"

"You have a family now. Might as well act like it. In a few years, the boys'll go off, just like you did, and—" his father made a slashing motion through the air "—all those chances to get to know each other are gone."

Luke's breath caught in his chest. Did he hear regret in his father's words?

"She's a cute little thing," his father continued. "You could do worse. In fact, you'd be hard-pressed to do better." He chuckled to himself. "Wonder what ol' Sheriff Forrester thinks about his new relations?"

"He likes his nephews a lot, from what I could tell."

"And you?"

"Me, not so much." Luke laughed ruefully. "He

doesn't seem too sure about me yet. I wonder how long he's known."

"Not long, I'd bet. Probably not much longer than you, because he and that rascal brother of his would have dragged you back here kicking and screaming to marry their sister shotgun-style. If I had to guess, I'd say that's why the big secret. She lived up north for years, you know."

"I really don't know much about Pepper," Luke murmured. "We went our separate ways after high school."

"I'd think your first reaction will be anger," his dad said, "but you've gotta admit she didn't try to tie you down."

"That doesn't excuse her not telling me."

"Would it have mattered, Luke?" his dad asked. "Or would you have been angry at being tied to Tulips?"

Luke didn't want to hear that, though the truth rang deep inside him. "I'm in too much shock to know what I would have wanted differently. What I have to do now is play the hand that's been dealt to me."

His father shifted in his recliner. "You've always been a lucky man. You'll manage."

It was time for a question he'd always wanted to ask. "When you say I'm lucky," Luke said, "you sound critical. Are you ashamed of me, Dad?"

His father looked at him. "At times I was."

They were silent for a long time. And then his dad spoke again. "Of course, if you're going to bring me grandkids, I'd probably be the proudest man on the planet."

Luke perked up. "Really?"

"Oh, hell, yeah," his father said. "I'm ready to get out of this damn chair. Grandkids will certainly do the trick."

Luke nodded, welcoming the healing seeping into the cracks of their relationship.

But starting over with Pepper—that was going to take a miracle.

PEPPER CURLED UP on her bed, worrying about Luke. Worrying about her boys. How would they take the knowledge that their father lived in this town—and that they'd just met him? She'd expected a lightning strike of recognition, but the boys didn't seem to suspect anything, and Luke hadn't pressed the issue of his fatherhood with them, for which she was grateful. Toby and Josh were making a smooth transition to life in Tulips. To throw a surprise father into the mix right now seemed like it might be too much at one time.

But Luke wasn't going to wait forever for them to know, and she didn't want him to. She just hoped she'd be ready when the moment happened.

She heard the doorbell chime. Throwing on a robe, she crept cautiously downstairs, wondering who might be visiting that wouldn't call first.

In the glow of the porch light, she could see Luke's broad shoulders. A powerful feeling shook her, but it didn't seem quite like relief, since she knew exactly why he was here. She opened the door. "Hi."

He nodded, his face drawn. "Were you in bed?"

"Not exactly. I couldn't sleep." She let him inside the house and closed the door before turning to face him. "Luke, thank you for not telling the boys, tonight."

"Actually, that's why I came by."

She swallowed. "All right. Please have a seat in the living room."

He went back to the floral sofa he'd found so inviting earlier, but didn't relax any more than he had before. "Where are the boys?"

"Fast asleep. Duke wears them out on the ranch. If he doesn't, Zach has a thousand things to occupy them with. They were worried about being bored in a small town, but that hasn't happened yet. By the time school starts in the fall, they'll be well-acclimated to Tulips."

Luke looked at her. "I think we should talk."

"All right."

"I suppose your brothers and the gang know I'm the father."

"I never told anyone, but…" She looked at him uncertainly. "I believe the likeness is telling. They figured it out."

"I would like to tell them myself."

"Of course," Pepper said softly. "I completely understand."

Luke nodded in appreciation. He glanced around the room slowly, noting each object before turning back to her. "I'm sorry that I didn't know you were pregnant. You must have been very scared, felt very alone."

Pepper didn't want to talk about the past. She'd

never let fear get the best of her. "Toby and Josh are awesome kids."

"You've done a good job with them. And become a doctor. It's a lot."

She stared at him silently.

"I haven't done much with my life, except be incredibly lucky," Luke said. "I figure this is my chance to prove myself."

"The boys won't expect you to do that," she said quickly. "Luke, they'll be thrilled to know their father."

He seemed comforted by the thought. "I hope so. Still, when they ask what I do for a living—"

"You'll say you own your own business," Pepper said, "and nothing else need be mentioned."

She was right. They didn't need a confessional; they needed a father who was there for them. That's what Luke had always wanted in his life. Even though he'd gotten the emotional support he craved later on, it had still felt good. "I'll try to be a good father."

She smiled. "I know you will."

Initially he'd been startled by his own father's suggestion that he, Pepper and the boys needed to be a family, but as the hours went by, he knew that was true. He wanted to give his boys his name. "Pepper," he said, "at the risk of being old school, I want to suggest something. Marry me."

She blinked. "Why?"

"Stability." He shrugged. "You lost your parents young, but you remember how good it felt to have a whole family. So do I."

He'd not planned any of the words coming from his mouth, but he meant every single one of them. Suddenly, it mattered that she understand what he felt his boys needed.

"Luke, I don't think—"

He reached to put a hand over hers. "Maybe we don't need to talk about marriage now. The back burner might be the best place for that subject until more things are settled with the boys. But I think it's worth considering."

Her eyes were so wide he could tell he'd startled her. No one was more startled than he. Less than a week ago, he'd been planning to take his job back from Hawk and Jellyfish and return to floating on the jewel-colored waters of the Greek Isles.

Sons. He'd change his whole life for his boys.

Chapter Nine

Pepper let Luke out, still in shock following his astonishing proposal. He kissed her forehead and left, seeming as bemused as she was by the fact that their lives were now inextricably intertwined.

She couldn't be sure how the boys would take it when they learned the truth. And the possibility of her marrying? She couldn't even guess how they might feel about that. Only time would tell, and for now, she needed to slow down enough to catch her breath.

Quietly, she went into the bedroom the boys had decided to share, each of them in a sleeping bag because she hadn't yet bought beds for their room. Duke had said she could take some from the Triple F, but they'd need beds there, too, so Pepper had decided to take the boys into Dallas soon and let them choose their own beds. Hopefully, decorating their room would help them feel that they had some control over their lives.

It seemed silly to think that painting a room and

choosing furniture might help them feel more secure about the move, when she was about to spring their father on them.

They slept deeply, unworried by the concerns plaguing her.

She left their room and went upstairs to lie down again, though she knew she wouldn't sleep. Marry Luke? The thought sent a delicious shiver up her spine in spite of herself. She told herself sternly that they'd never work as a married couple. They were too different. It would be stressful on Toby and Josh because they would want to see their parents get along.

Though the picture Luke had painted was a pretty one—a complete family—she reluctantly admitted she wanted to marry for love. Maybe that was an unlikely dream, but her heart demanded it. Otherwise, marriage for her would just be signing another contract, as she had for this house and her clinic.

Love. That was the only reason she would marry.

And she knew too well that Luke McGarrett was not in love with her.

"IT'S A START," Helen said to Pansy as they examined a drawing for a giant cake that Valentine from Union Junction proposed to make for them. "It could certainly feed a hundred hungry bachelors." She glanced up as Pepper walked in carrying a box of pink plastic glasses. "Check out this cake, Pepper. Valentine has offered to bake a celebratory kickoff cake for our upcoming Fishing For Bachelors extravaganza."

Pepper smiled as she looked at the sketch. "Beautiful as always, Valentine."

Helen thought Pepper hadn't looked too hard at the cake or she might have noticed it seemed a bit phallic in structure. Pansy was no help in this matter due to her macular degeneration—hard to see the whole drawing, Helen figured—so she was counting on Pepper to perhaps suggest Valentine could scale the design a bit differently.

Or maybe she was simply being too hypercritical of an artistic vision. She did so want everything to go well for their first big town project, especially since Duke had put up so many objections. Bug was looking forward to his parade; Hiram was anticipating his many sundry jobs. Helen thought Pepper's boys might get a real boost out of seeing folks in a small town working together on something fun.

She worried about those boys.

"I think the cake is beautiful," Pepper said, looking at the drawing more carefully, "though I wonder if maybe a wide rectangle shape might be better."

Valentine nodded. "I could do that. Or even round with tulips on it."

Helen smiled. "You're a genius, Valentine. That would be a cake to remember." She was definitely getting old, she decided, if cakes were taking on puzzling shapes.

"I believe the Malfunction Junction brothers who are in town want to be included in the fun," Valentine said. "As helping hands, of course, not fishers of women."

"Funny," Helen said. "By the way, thank your husband for offering up his brothers. We sure could use the help with organizing boats and things. Weigh-in could be tricky, too." The big day was only two weeks away. She wanted everything to go as smooth as a ribbon. Some towns had tractor pulls, some had pumpkin-growing contests, some even had weed-whacker races and town fairs. All she wanted was one afternoon where lots of available fellows could see Tulips and its talented, special ladies.

She planned to ask someone to take Toby and Josh out to cast a few lures for fish, though not women. The boys would enjoy an afternoon on a lake with a role model. Of course, the obvious choice was Luke, but she daren't meddle, she told herself with a glance at Pepper.

Valentine and Pepper laughed at something Helen hadn't heard, and then Valentine left with her drawing, excited to get home and redo her design.

Pepper looked at Helen and Pansy, and it seemed all the joy went out of her eyes. "I could really use some advice," she said.

Pansy wheeled the tea tray over. "Have some fortifying tea," she offered. "Valentine brought us some new scones she's trying out."

Helen sat, feeling the skin on her arm begin to itch, in that one place that always bothered her whenever she felt nervous. "We're not much good with advice, but we're happy to listen."

Pepper didn't touch the scone or the tea, although

the tempting treats sat in front of her just in case. "Luke knows."

"Knows what, dear?" Pansy said.

"That he is Toby's and Josh's father." Pepper sighed. "And you don't have to act like you didn't know, because I know you guessed."

"Do the boys know?" Helen asked.

"I don't think so," Pepper said slowly. "They seemed fine this morning, didn't mention Luke at all. Didn't even ask why I'd introduced him to them."

"I think that's strange right there," Helen said. "Kids always ask questions, usually at the most inconvenient times."

Pepper considered that. "We're pretty close. I feel they would have said something."

"Maybe not, if they were afraid of scaring Luke off," Pansy mused. "They're twins. They would think deeply and discuss the matter and try to make things easier on everyone."

"I never thought about that," Pepper said slowly.

"So what do you need our advice on, dear?" Helen asked. "It seems you already have everything in hand."

"I don't," she said. "I was trying to think of the best way Luke and I could tell the boys without upsetting them. There's no book on this subject, no body of research to refer to."

Helen nodded. "Not everything is as cut-and-dried as looking in a medical journal."

"Act on your instinct," Pansy said. "I bet you've developed wonderful instincts during your years of practice."

"Not for this." Pepper looked at her friends. "I want them to have an easy transition here. I didn't figure Luke into this mix. Not right now."

"You'd be surprised how things sometime happen for a reason," Helen said, "and sometimes work out for the best. How did Luke take to seeing himself in double?"

Pepper thought back over his reaction. "At first he was completely dumbfounded. And he was very angry with me, of course. He will be for a long time, I'm sure. Then, he asked me to marry him."

Astonished, Helen clapped her hands. "What did you say?"

"Oh," Pepper said, "I was too surprised to say much of anything at the time. And though I admit that I'm at the age where settling down as a family is appealing, Luke and I...well, no."

Pansy patted her arm. "He's a cute devil, you have to admit."

Pepper laughed. "And I obviously thought so fourteen years ago. However, it just wouldn't work. I got myself through undergrad in three years, and medical school with honors, and backpacked through Europe with my kids and Aunt Jerry and started my own practice. I feel pretty well versed in what can be done and what can't." She hesitated before smiling shyly. "I think marrying for love works best, rather than knitting our family together just for the sake of the classic fairy tale."

"I don't know," Helen said. "I like the classics."

Pepper laughed. "You're a softie. And a romantic." She stood. "I love you both. Thank you for your help. I have to go get another load of glasses."

"But we didn't help," Pansy said. "I feel certain we never offered a word of advice."

"I feel better just talking about everything," Pepper said, "and now I know I made the right decision in telling Luke no. Talking it over with you cemented my decision."

"But I thought we were advising on how best to tell the twins the wonderful news," Helen said.

Pepper nodded. "You gave me the answer," she said, looking more peaceful. "I simply need to trust in my boys."

Helen watched her leave before turning to Pansy. "He asked her to marry him!"

"I know!" Pansy giggled. "He's turned out to be such a good boy."

"Who would have thought?" Helen considered the surprising news. "Luke McGarrett wanting to settle down. Even I didn't think discovering he was a father would have that effect on him."

"My bet is he still has a soft spot for Pepper," Pansy said, and Helen nodded.

"It's obvious to see why. She's beautiful, smart, talented—"

"The mother of his children," Pansy interjected.

"That's the kicker," Helen agreed. "But I still didn't imagine him proposing this soon, nor perhaps even at all. He's always been such a rapscallion."

"I don't know," Pansy mused, "sometimes those are the best men to catch. Look at Hiram and Bug.

They haven't always been model men, but they're pretty steady now."

"They're old as the hills!" Helen said. "Pepper couldn't wait that long for Luke to figure out what a good thing he has sitting right under his nose."

"Do you think they'll fall in love?"

"I think," Helen said carefully, "that given a boat on the water and fishing poles with no bait and a motor that gives out, *anything* could happen."

"I thought we wanted Luke to have a day with his sons," Pansy said.

"There's time for that," her friend said, "but if Luke really wants to marry Pepper, I say June is a lovely month for a wedding."

"We're going to have to get working on our stubborn doctor," Pansy murmured, and Helen nodded.

"Exactly the plan."

LUKE FELT AS if he was going to explode. He had to tell his sons that he was their father. Somehow, it seemed he'd waited all his life for just this moment. He was impatient not to lose another second of father-son bonding.

He felt he should be mad at Pepper for not telling him sooner—and he had been soul-deep angry—but he couldn't deny that he wouldn't have been much of a father as a teenager. Or even as a twenty-year-old.

But he was ready now.

He was also ready, he was shocked to discover, for marriage.

Pepper hadn't seemed thrilled with his proposal,

but that was all right for now. Life moved slowly in Tulips—he knew that as well as anyone. Plus, she'd been on her own for a long time, doing just fine without him, thank you very much.

It was up to him to fit into her world, in order to form that family he envisioned.

"Did you ask her?" his father asked.

Luke thought it interesting that his dad no longer sat in his recliner except to watch the news at night. Other than that program, the TV stayed off. Today, his father had kept himself busy watering the dried-out grass at the front of the property. He'd cleared some stray branches and twigs that had fallen during the winter. Then he'd taken paper towels, the hose and a bucket of soapy water out to clean the windows.

"I did ask her," Luke said, "but it didn't come out as much of a proposal. More of a business proposition."

His father grunted. "Which she was lady enough to turn down."

"Yeah." Luke grinned. "I just need practice. I've never done this before."

"I wouldn't worry about one misfire. At least she knows you respect her. The rest will follow."

"That easy?" Luke wasn't certain where Pepper was concerned.

"Yeah. She's a good girl. But very traditional, despite being so successful. She'll want love."

Luke blinked. *Love?* It was too soon to think about that, wasn't it? "Dad, you may be overconfident. We were both young. She was left in a bad situation with difficult choices. I don't know if love grows under those circumstances. Maybe the best we can hope for is mutual respect."

His father tossed a sponge into his bucket. "Don't be a quitter, son. At least open the gate before you decide you can't run through it." He gazed at the windows he'd just washed. "And I guess you're smart enough to wear a condom if you ever got a second chance."

"Actually," Luke said, "I was wearing a condom then, if I remember correctly. I recall it not staying on as well as it could have."

"At least you have some sense." His father turned to attack another window. "I can't wait to meet my grandsons. I'm trying to be patient, but it's hard."

"I can't wait to tell them," Luke said, meaning every word. "I'm going to have to go very slowly with Pepper so that she'll know I'm here to stay in my sons' lives."

"Good plan," his father said, and Luke hoped he was right.

Chapter Ten

Pepper and Luke chose a night a week later to tell the boys, when they'd given themselves a bit more time to think through how best to present the truth to them. "I'm so afraid they're going to be upset," Pepper told Luke as they sat on her front porch a few minutes before Duke was set to drop the kids off.

"I'm afraid they're not going to want me," Luke admitted.

She looked at him. "Why wouldn't they?"

"Why would they?" He pushed a hand through his hair. "They've gotten along all this time without me. They have your brothers as role models and Bug and Hiram for backup."

"That's not the same as one's very own father," Pepper murmured. She knew how the boys had longed to know who their father was over the years, and how she'd had to skirt the question without hurting them. "I'm glad it's almost over," she said slowly. "I'm scared they'll be angry with me for not telling them sooner."

Luke was aware of how he and his dad hadn't gotten along over the years. Would the boys look forward to having him as a father? "We all do the best we can and make the most appropriate decisions possible under trying circumstances. I think you've done a helluva job."

She appreciated his forgiving attitude. "Luke, I've never told you how thankful I am that you're taking this well. I know you had to have been angry. You have every right to be. I'll never know whether I made the right choices or not, but I feel very blessed that you seem to be welcoming the boys instead of turning away."

He put a hand over hers. "Pepper, I could no more turn away from them—or you—than I could my own soul."

Her breath caught. "Thank you," she whispered.

"Actually, I thank you. You gave me something I never knew I needed." He put an arm around her shoulders in a nonsexual manner and quietly said, "I wish I hadn't said that I didn't think I could ever forgive you."

"Oh." Pepper put her head on his shoulder. "Your actions later spoke louder than your words. I understood."

They sat silently for a few moments, cherishing the gentle moment of friendship they shared.

Duke drove up with the boys, parking his big truck so they could get out. Toby and Josh jumped out to greet their mom and manfully shake hands with Luke, who'd stood as soon as they saw Duke's truck. Pepper waved at her brother, who waved back, then drove off without getting out.

He was trying to give them privacy, and Pepper loved him for his support.

"Did you have fun, boys?" she asked.

"Uncle Duke is pretty fun," Toby said as they walked inside. "We like him a lot."

Pepper had them all sit at the kitchen table, exactly as she and Luke had planned. There were cookies waiting, and milk, and some tea and tissues just in case. Pepper was certain that after all the years of pent-up secrecy, she was going to bawl just from relief.

God, please let this go well.

"Boys," she said slowly, "you know how much I love you."

"Oh, Mom," Josh said, "don't get mushy on us in front of Mr. Luke, please." Toby nodded with an embarrassed glance at Luke.

"Well, I do," Pepper continued. "And Mr. Luke and I feel tonight is a good night for us to tell you something."

Toby grinned. "You're getting married."

Josh laughed. "You're gonna owe me five bucks, Toby. He didn't think you would, Mom. Toby thought you were way too busy with the clinic."

Pepper frowned to cover her embarrassment that her boys had brought up the *M* word. "First of all, no betting allowed. Second, no betting on family members."

"Yes, Mom," the boys murmured, completely mortified to be called down in front of Luke. They glanced at him again and he gave them a half smile designed to show he understood, but that he also agreed with their mother.

Pepper took a deep breath. "You've asked me for years about your father. Boys—" Her voice broke. She couldn't say the words and she didn't know why. *I'm so afraid. Everything is going to change. I don't want them hurt.*

"Toby, Josh," Luke said quietly, "I'm your father."

Toby looked at Josh. "Told ya."

Pepper blinked. "Told you what?"

"That Mr. Luke was our dad. We look just like him," Josh explained. "Except he's old, of course."

A weight slid into Pepper's stomach. "Why didn't you say something to me if that's what you thought?"

Josh shrugged. "Because we didn't want you to cry. You usually cry when we talk about stuff like that."

"Oh." Pepper glanced at Luke, who was looking at her with a puzzled expression. "Well, Mr. Luke— I mean, your father—would like to spend some time getting to know you better."

"And I'd like to introduce you to your grandfather," Luke said, neatly picking up the story. "He's very excited about meeting you."

Josh said, "Oh, cool."

Toby added, "Is he here?"

"Just a few blocks away." Luke grinned.

"So," Josh said slowly, "does this mean we call you Dad now?"

"If you want," Luke replied.

"It may be kind of weird," Toby said, "I sort of forgot about wanting a dad. I knew we had one, we just figured you'd never come around."

"Well," Luke stated, his eyes meeting Pepper's in a quick stab of sympathy, "I've come around now. And I'll be around forever."

They looked at him for a long time, then Josh slid his hand across the table for Luke to shake. "Nice to meet you, Dad."

"Yeah," Toby said, doing the same. "You're better than I figured you'd be."

"Oh?" Startled, Luke raised an eyebrow.

"Yeah. When Mom dated—and that wasn't much—she always brought home nerds."

Luke glanced at Pepper.

"College professors," she quickly said. "Remember, I spent a lot of time on campus."

"It's cool you're not a nerd," Josh agreed. "They were boring."

Luke laughed, feeling a little relieved that Pepper hadn't been dating handsome, eligible doctors. On the other hand, a little spurt of jealousy shot through him that she'd been dating, at all. These were his sons! He didn't want to think about another man buddying up to them in order to woo their mother.

He'd deal with the dragon of jealousy, later. "I'm really proud to be your father."

Josh grinned. "So, guess you have to do all the dad stuff with us now."

Luke recognized bait and grabbed it gladly. "Like?"

"Girls, for starters," Toby said. "Mom never let us around any. If it wasn't for school, we'd never know even one."

No shock there, considering there'd been no father in the home to guide them. "The teen years are soon enough to start thinking about girls. You didn't miss anything before now. They don't get super-cute until they're, like—" he glanced at Pepper, who was staring at him, and decided to tweak her a little "—thirty."

"Gross!" Toby made a face.

"We'll have a prom before then," Josh said.

Luke laughed. "Is there another subject you think dads ought to be good with, besides girls?" By the tiny scowl on Pepper's face, he figured it was best to choose another topic.

"We don't know," Toby said.

Luke nodded, gazing at his sons. "It's okay. We'll work on it together. It'll be fun that way."

They grinned at him and Luke had a sudden vision that family was his new calling in life— thanks to Pepper.

THE BOYS went to bed a few hours later. Pepper walked Luke to the front door, relieved and torn at the same time. "Thank you for making that as easy as possible."

"I thought we did well," Luke agreed. "But you raised fine kids, Pepper. They're calm. Like you."

She warmed from his praise. "Their aunt Jerry is pretty capable, too."

"So can I take them to meet Dad, tomorrow?"

"Of course," Pepper said quickly. She wanted to go as well, but didn't feel right about intruding. After all, Luke deserved some time alone with his boys as they got to know each other.

"Want to come, too?"

She glanced up at him, thinking he really was a handsome, caring man despite all the rumors of his wild ways. "Oh, no," she murmured, "you and your dad need time with Toby and Josh."

"It would probably feel more normal to them if you were there. They're calm kids, I know, but it still helps to have your mom around sometimes."

She smiled, recognizing he was trying hard to appeal to her sentimental side. "Do you always get what you want?"

He touched her cheek. "If I think it's right, I work pretty hard at it."

A shock of sexual desire hit her unexpectedly and hotly, deep in the core of her body. The feeling stunned her, and a long-slumbering flower of lust bloomed. She stared at Luke, her eyes wide with wonder. It felt so good that she didn't want it to cease.

His palm slipped down her cheek to caress her chin, a gentle introduction of his flesh to hers, a feeling of sensuous possession. It was so different, so unlike what they'd known before, that Pepper was riveted, wanting to feel more.

"Pepper?" he said huskily.

He wasn't looking for a reply, but permission, she realized, her body heating with excitement. He would leave her alone, remove his hand, if she only said—

"Yes," she replied softly, giving him the permission she knew he was craving. So Luke bent his head and kissed her deeply, hotly, the way a man kissed a woman he wanted.

And Pepper knew she wanted him just this way. After all these years, it felt good—right—to be kissed by Luke.

She felt like an angel, Luke decided, drawing Pepper to him tightly so he could taste her more deeply. He'd known attraction many times, but this was different. This was a soul-deep connection making him hungry for everything he could learn of her mouth, her body, her emotions. What made her happy, what made her sad.

He was going to spend every day of his life learning how to make her happy. He'd been given a family: sons, a father, the mother of his children. Pulling Pepper more tightly to him, Luke molded his body against hers, feeling how perfectly they fit together. *This is the real meaning of lucky.*

Pepper pulled away from him slowly and he let her go—for now.

Chapter Eleven

Luke talked Pepper into going to his dad's with the boys, using the irresistible lure that Toby and Josh would probably like her moral support. It had to be difficult to meet one's grandfather for the first time, he'd told her, when the children never knew they had a living grandparent. This was all true enough, but the bottom line was Luke wanted Pepper with him.

The more he kissed her, the more he craved her.

It was a really strange phenomenon for a bachelor with freedom deeply embedded in his soul. He glanced at Pepper, who sat beside him. Shapely legs showed beneath a flared skirt he thought was perhaps a little old-fashioned, but typical of Pepper—she did like the mother role, and certainly no teenager would be caught dead in that skirt. A white blouse left her arms bare and gave her a fresh, cool appearance. She wore her dark hair up on her head, and no makeup that he could see—a planned strategy by most women, but in Pepper's case, he was pretty certain he was looking at the genuine article.

He caught himself gazing at her maybe every other second when he was with her. With Toby and Josh in the backseat, he tried not to stare, but his eyes were prisoners to her allure.

His dad's idea of making a family with Pepper kept buzzing around in Luke's mind. They'd already made the family, he amended; now he needed to convince her that they could be lovers again. Only this time he wouldn't be the green boy who couldn't keep the condom adjusted, and she'd be all woman. The girl had been sweet, but the woman… The thought set him on high heat.

"We're here, boys," he said, stopping the truck. They scrambled out to look around with interest as his father stepped out on the porch. Children and grandfather stared at each other for a long time, sizing each other up. Luke thought about how brave these boys were being, and how many changes they were assimilating at such a fast pace. He was proud of them and couldn't wait to get to know them better.

Without being prodded, they walked up on the porch, solemnly shaking their grandfather's hand. Luke's dad nodded, recognizing that hugs weren't coming yet, but the smile on his face said he didn't care. He'd dressed in his best clothes, as if he was going to church, and Luke could smell barbecue cooking at the back of the house.

"Hi, Dad," he said, giving him a hug. "This is Toby and Josh. Boys, this is your grandfather."

They looked at one another again, trying to decide what they all might mean to each other at this point in their lives. "There are three-wheelers out back, if your dad says it's okay," the older man said, and the boys whooped, waiting long enough for Luke's nod before tearing off to inspect them.

"You'll have to ride with them," his dad said to Luke and Pepper. "At first, to show them the safety rules."

"Three-wheelers? Dad." Luke grinned. "Did you rob a bank?"

"It was a small thing to do for ones grandkids." He gave Pepper a kiss on the cheek. "'Bout time you showed up again. Some kind of doc you're turning out to be."

Pepper smiled at the teasing complaint. "I did bring my stethoscope and cuff, Mr. McGarrett."

"I figured you would. By the way, my name's Bill."

"All right. Bill." Pepper glanced at Luke, and he grinned.

"Guess he doesn't mind your stethoscope anymore."

Bill headed around to the back, with an energy in every step that hadn't been there a week before. "Come on, you two. You have to see the three-wheelers. I'm taking pictures. I've decided to take up photography."

Now that I've got a family to photograph, were the unspoken words.

Gratitude filled Luke; regret for the days when father and son might have been closer ebbed away. He was in the here and now—all he needed was to convince Pepper that the here and now was heaven.

From the stiffness in her posture as she watched her boys inspect the ATV's, he knew it wouldn't be easy. He was going to have to go slow and gentle to win her. This time, he couldn't count on luck.

PEPPER HAD GROWN UP on a ranch. She knew all about off-roading, and three-wheeling, and mud-dogging and even hot air balloons on special occasions. Kites, roller skating off the back end of a truck, campouts in the truck bed to stare up at the stars with friends and family—those were the benefits of living on a lot of land in the country.

But she wasn't ready for her boys to be three-wheeling. As a doctor, she knew it was dangerous; as a mother, she was scared. But she sensed their world was changing, and that a man's ways, thought processes and even his toys would be beneficial to her sons' teen years—if she could unclench her knuckles long enough to enjoy the fact that they were having a lot of fun getting to know their father.

But Luke brought other dangers that made her nervous. She'd been reckless falling into his arms last night, kissing and being kissed as if they were erasing a time lag that no longer mattered.

It did matter. She didn't know Luke, and he didn't know her, despite their mutual parenting bond. It would be too easy to fall into playing house because the most wonderful components, the parts she'd always wanted, were already in place: the boys, Bill, her family, her home and clinic.

Something cautioned her that falling into a pattern of family would bring heartbreak to all of them, eventually. She wouldn't let the boys be hurt by unrealistic expectations. They hadn't said it, but they wouldn't be human if they didn't want their family pieced together to make a whole. It was the essential image of *The Waltons, Happy Days* and *Leave It To Beaver.*

But real life usually wasn't that neat and orderly. Certainly it hadn't been for her. She'd gotten by on strength and determination.

She watched Luke instruct the boys on how to turn on and off the engines and how to avoid a spill. He had certainly embraced fatherhood, she had to admit. She'd worried he might want nothing to do with his sons; in retrospect, that worry seemed unfair to him.

Still, she knew of his reputation. He couldn't have changed his spots so much. Could he?

She sat on a wooden bench next to Bill as he fiddled with his new camera.

"Fun to watch 'em, isn't it?" he asked.

His joy pulled a smile from her. "I can never get enough of them. Maybe that's too much a mom thing, but they're good kids. They get in the occasional scrape, but nothing I can't handle."

The words hung in the air and Pepper regretted them almost as soon as she'd spoken. Of course, Mr. McGarrett would want his son to have shared those times with the twins.

But Bill just nodded. "The Bible-thumpers came to see me last night."

"Bible-thumpers?"

"Yeah." Grinning, he squeezed off a shot of Toby riding with Luke for a trial run. "Trying to tell me the boys need to be in school in the fall."

"I know they need to be in school!" Pepper exclaimed, outraged. "I have a few degrees, myself!"

He laughed and patted her hand. "I think their complaint was with me, not you. In fact, I think the school question was their excuse to get in my front door. They're very proud of that new school your family built."

Pepper nodded. "Education is important."

"Forresters are good for this town. And I think the Bible-thumpers—that would be Ms. Pansy and Ms. Helen—wanted to make certain I planned to meet the standard."

"Standard?" Pepper looked at him curiously.

"They want me in church," he said with a put-upon sigh and a twinkle in his eyes. "I do believe the school issue was a cover for getting me churched."

"Oh," Pepper said.

He nodded. "The little one—Pansy—she said as long as it was any institution of faith, that'd be good for my soul. For the boys' sake, of course." He laughed to himself. "I don't think the ol' gal was as worried about my salvation as she is about my reputation where these kids are concerned."

Pepper didn't know what to think of that. She watched Josh take his instructional turn with Luke, and Bill squeezed off another picture.

"I think I'll join them," he said, and Pepper looked at him.

"Join them?"

"The Tulips Saloon Gang."

"Oh," Pepper said, "they got to you."

"They've been trying to get to me for years," he admitted. "But it was just easier to sit in my den and be mad. Mad at myself, mad at Luke, mad at the world." He shrugged. "Then you came along and everything changed."

"I hope you'll forgive me for not letting you get to know the boys sooner."

"Well," he said, "I think I'll appreciate them more now. I've been down to the pits of hell and back. Not appreciating family ties has cost me dearly." He polished his camera lens. "Second chances are just as good as first, if you learned something."

Pepper figured that applied to her life, as well. "I hope I'm learning something."

"You are," Bill said. "So this gang of busybodies may have a new member, for the boys' sake. I want my grandsons to see that I'm living right."

She laughed. "That would be for your sake, not the boys, right? The cookies and pies too much to resist?"

"Think my doctor would frown on too much of that." He looked at her. "You know in *Gone With the Wind,* how Rhett Butler sucks up to the old biddies so that his daughter, Bonnie, will have entrée into the best circles?"

"Yes," Pepper said, amused.

"Think I best keep up my side of the family tree," he said.

She smiled. "There's nothing wrong with your side of the tree."

"I hope you'll remember that," Bill said. "They're

betting in town on you and Luke. The odds are that you won't marry my boy. In horse racing, that's called a long shot, also referred to as an outsider."

The smile faded from Pepper's face. "You slipped that into the conversation very neatly," she observed. "You may be conniving enough to be in the gang."

"Nothing wrong with conniving," Bill said, "as long as you do it with a pure heart."

She raised her brows. "I'm going to tell Pansy and Helen they can't preach to you about church and take bets on my life at the same time."

Just then the boys roared off on their inaugural solo three-wheeler ride, Luke watching them protectively.

"Don't know that Pansy and Helen participated in the betting, just the reporting. But I'd like you to think about it, all the same," Bill said. "I've always been one to go against the odds. I figure you have, too."

"I'm not sure what we're talking about."

"You want the best for your sons, and I want the best for my grandsons. Now, I'm not saying my boy's the best thing for you, necessarily. I'm merely asking you not to listen to gossip."

"Gossip?"

"Well, the odds are long, apparently, because supposedly you're far too sensible to ever consider a man with a wandering foot. And so on and so forth. You know how people talk, even with the best of intentions." Bill leaned back, relaxing as he watched Luke run after his sons. "You may think I'm being presumptuous, and I am, but I also thought you'd want to know what's being said about your family.

Not that public opinion would influence you. Still, information is power in a small town, as I'm sure you know."

Pepper noted the "your family," understanding that he was trying to give her her space. He was right on many counts. "You're saying if you can turn over a new leaf, perhaps I can, too."

"And Luke," he reminded her. "We're all in this for the kids, in my humble, unasked-for, opinion."

"*So* humble." She laughed, not as offended as she'd been preparing to be. *So sneaky, so smooth. Like father, like son.*

Chapter Twelve

"We like him," Toby and Josh told Pepper later that night, when they were all sitting in front of the TV watching a *Bonanza* rerun.

Pepper glanced up. "Your father?"

They nodded.

"I'm glad." She looked at them carefully. They seemed to be telling the truth, not just saying it because they thought she wanted to hear it. "It's the three-wheelers, right?"

"That helped," Josh said. "We were afraid he'd be one of those strict, bossy dads."

"Or a busy dad," Toby said. "The kind that's always in a suit and tie. And that doesn't have time to do anything but work."

"What does he do, anyway?" Josh asked.

"I don't completely know," Pepper said. She knew very little about the years Luke had been away from Tulips. "You could ask him."

"So could you," Toby said, and Pepper shook her head.

"Don't you like him?" Josh asked.

I knew this was coming. She took a deep breath. "I like Luke. But you know what? We're different people than we were." She ruffled their hair fondly. "Now we can be good friends because of you two."

Toby and Josh considered that for a moment.

"It's okay with us if you decide to like him more than that," Josh finally said, speaking their combined opinion.

Pepper shook her head again. "I'm glad you like Luke. I'm sure he wants to be a good father and will try real hard." She thought about what she wanted to say next. "Thank you for not being mad at me for not telling you sooner."

"We liked living close to Aunt Jerry," Toby said slowly. "We always knew we had a dad. We just didn't think he would want to know us."

Pepper thought about that, too. She hadn't wanted her boys to be hurt, to feel the harsh sting of rejection that could last a lifetime.

"If Dad asked you to marry him, would you?" Josh queried, and Pepper's heart constricted. She couldn't admit that Luke *had* asked her—a hasty proposal from a man in shock at learning that he had children. They would have regretted it later if she'd taken him seriously.

But if he truly wanted to marry her?

She gave the safe answer. "We don't know each other well enough to consider marriage," she said gently. "You'll understand that later in your own lives. The person you marry should be your best friend."

They glanced at each other.

"A girl could never be my best friend," Toby said confidently, and Josh nodded in agreement.

They had each other, and that was best friend enough. Pepper smiled. "When you start school, you'll make lots of new friends."

"Will we be Forrester or McGarrett?" Toby wondered. "I mean, since our dad lives here and all, it would be pretty weird not to be McGarrett."

Pepper stared at her boys, her stomach cramping suddenly. They had a point. This was something she hadn't considered, and didn't want to, now. "I don't know," she murmured.

"We'd like the kids to know we have a dad, Mom," Josh said, his tone practical.

"And we'd like them to know that Luke is our dad," Toby added.

Pepper put her hands over her face. It was all moving too fast. "Does Luke know you're asking me about this?"

"No," they said.

After a moment, she told herself to take a deep breath and relax. She put her hands in her lap and went into professional mode. "While I think your question is well thought out, I need a little time to think about it myself. It simply hadn't occurred to me that you… I mean, it's something to consider." She didn't want the boys to see how surprised she was. And yet, their concern and their question were certainly valid. But Luke had some say in this, too. It was his name, after all.

"We could ask him," Toby offered, not aware of the implications of what he was saying.

Pepper shook her head. "No, thank you, sweetie. I'll talk to your dad and see what he thinks is best."

They smiled, relieved. "We really would like the kids in school to know we have a dad. Since we do have one," Josh pointed out, and Pepper nodded.

"I understand. I'll talk to him."

Bonanza's hired hands got themselves out of a fix on the TV screen, and they all laughed as their dog outwitted the bad guys.

"We wouldn't mind a dog, too," Toby said, and Pepper picked up a pillow to pretend to smack her twins. *And a white picket fence, and a Betty Crocker mom and a happy ending to boot.*

Still, it was what she'd had growing up, and she completely understood their dreams. But how Luke fit into those dreams she wasn't certain.

All she knew was that he kissed like a dream.

PEPPER TOOK THE BOYS to the Tulips Saloon so she could visit, and also to let everyone know that betting on her and Luke wasn't necessary.

"It's more fun to bet on something that's not a sure thing," Pepper pointed out, "but I thought I'd let you know there's no romance budding between Luke and me."

Pansy and Helen nodded. Pansy dropped a lump of sugar in Pepper's tea and Helen laid out some cookies. The boys had found Duke's golden retriever,

Molly, and decided to walk with her around the town square, the dog leading the way.

"We figured there wasn't," Pansy said, "but you know how the fellows are. They take bets on whether it's going to rain, and that's definitely not a sure thing around here."

Pepper sighed, realizing the futility of reasoning with her friends. "So, just a few more days until the 'big fish.'"

"We can't wait," Pansy said. "I declare, I've never had this much fun planning anything!"

"We got fifty entries," Helen said. "Fifty! Can you imagine fifty bachelors around here? The girls will go crazy." She squinted through her black-rimmed spectacles at a sheet of paper. "Now, we have you scheduled for boat number four."

"Me?" Pepper put her cookie down. "I'm not entered."

"Of course you are, dear. We would never leave a daughter of Tulips out. Even if it were a debutante ball, we'd be sure to invite you as a chaperone."

"But I don't want a man," Pepper insisted. If she did, she'd be more inclined to look at the father of her children.

But Helen shook her head. "It's just good clean fun, not a marriage proposal. We're trying to show off the town, not our females. Now, if a girl was to catch a man out on that lake, we certainly wouldn't be unhappy about that. But we're casting Tulips' lures next weekend."

Pepper wasn't certain. She didn't trust these two

sweet ladies not to try to set her up. Tulips or not, she didn't want to be stuck all day in a boat with a groper, which she figured would be just her luck. "I'll swim to shore," she told them, just as the door opened and Luke walked in.

"Swimming? Are we going swimming?" he asked, coming over to kiss Pansy and Helen on the cheek. "My boys are out there running after a dog," he told Pepper, announcing to the whole world—or at least everyone in the room—that Toby and Josh were his children.

"Pansy and Helen have put me in boat number four for next weekend's Man Catch," Pepper complained, and the ladies laughed.

"Did we call it a Man Catch?" Pansy asked Helen.

"I believe we might have," she replied innocently.

Luke scowled but didn't say anything.

"Luke, can I talk to you?" Pepper asked. When he nodded, she said, "Excuse me. I'll be right back, ladies."

"Take your time," Pansy said. "We're going to try a new kind of frosting on some cookies for next weekend. They're fish shaped, but we're not sure if we like the texture."

Pepper barely heard them as she followed Luke outside. He was so breathtakingly handsome, she found it hard to believe that the two of them had created children. The more time he spent in Tulips, the less continental and the more Western he became, a very sexy look for him. Gazing up into his dark eyes, she told herself to be brave. "The boys mentioned something to me I hadn't considered before."

Luke raised his brows, his eyes glittering. "Such as?"

This was difficult, Pepper told herself. No one could help her with this question; in the interest of keeping their family matters private, she'd decided to talk to Luke and only Luke about the boys' request. "The twins asked me last night about…"

She couldn't say it. Giving her children his last name would be forever sharing them with Luke. As long as they had her name, they seemed to be hers, and hers alone, just as they'd been for thirteen years. "They were wondering about your last name."

He waited, his gaze still.

"Your last name and them," she said, feeling awkward. "I didn't know how you'd feel about that. I told them I'd mention it to you, but I understand—"

She stopped stumbling over words when his hand closed on her wrist. Then a trembling started that deep breathing couldn't subside. *It's discussing the boys that's making me nervous—not Luke,* she told herself.

"Pepper, you're so knotted up you're making me jumpy. Are you saying they want to be McGarretts?" he asked.

"Yes," she whispered, tugging her arm away.

"Well." He scratched his chin, thinking. "There's only two ways for that to happen. One, we get married. Two, I'm sure there's legal paperwork to be filed for a name change. I'm sure your brother Duke knows. Or someone around this den of conspirators does. They've probably already looked it up."

She felt a need to explain. "It's just that with school starting in the fall—"

"You don't need to go into it," Luke said. "It's perfectly natural, and in fact, better for them. Unless you have an objection."

Too quickly, she shook her head, denying herself the painful emotions racing through her. "It will be hard not to think of them as Toby and Josh Forrester. But I do understand." She looked at Luke. "And part of me is glad."

"Part?" He cupped her chin. "This is hard for you, isn't it?"

"Yes," Pepper admitted, "and I'm ashamed of that."

"Don't be," he said, pulling her into his arms for a close, nonthreatening hug. "You're being very brave."

She didn't feel brave. Pepper put her face against Luke's chest, fighting to get a grip on the wild feelings surging through her—and caught the scent of his skin, the smell of the laundry detergent he used and the heat of his body. It was like standing still in a place she'd never been, only realizing it felt strangely, wonderfully familiar.

Like home.

Chapter Thirteen

"I should have been there for you," Luke said. "I have responsibility in this, too." He wasn't proud that he'd made love to Pepper and then left town without even a goodbye. A man couldn't blame that on teenage mistakes. He wouldn't want his teenagers to use that excuse, or behave that way.

Toby and Josh were only four years younger now than Luke and Pepper had been when they created them. It was time to start facing his life if he really wanted to present a good role model for his sons to follow.

He wanted that more than anything.

"I'm sorry I left you behind," he told Pepper, pulling away from her. They began to walk down the street in the direction he'd seen the boys and dog joyfully heading. "Pepper, I should've phoned you. At the very least I should have called to see if you were all right." He took a deep breath, glad that he was finally making this confession. "I'm sorry I didn't. It was a jerky thing to do."

"It's probably turned out better this way. No regrets. At least I never had any."

He wondered about that. How could a young girl not be afraid of facing motherhood alone? "I don't know. I think you're giving me the light version of the story." He had a feeling she must have been very scared, not to even tell her brothers. Or Pansy and Helen. Pepper seemed pretty close to those two. "We should start over," he said.

"We are," she murmured.

"Yeah. I guess so." They walked half a block before he spoke again. "You're even more beautiful than you were before."

She laughed. "I was never beautiful. Other girls in the class, yes. Me? No."

"The most beautiful bookworm I ever saw. I always admired your intelligence. I still do."

When she glanced up at him, he shrugged. "I haven't done anything with my life that requires great concentration and brains, not like getting a medical degree or raising twins."

"The boys were wondering what you do for a living," Pepper said. "I didn't know what to tell them."

"My last job was working as a bodyguard for three beautiful women," Luke said, "but that's not a good answer for my young sons."

Pepper stopped, staring up at him. "A bodyguard?"

He shrugged. "It was an accidental job that worked out."

"I can't see you standing outside dressing rooms

while women try on clothes, or watching while they eat."

He grinned. "It was more of a terrorism gig. I kept an eye on a general and his family."

"His beautiful family."

"Uh-huh." He tugged at her hair. "That's the same tone I used when I heard you were going out in a boat with a strange guy for the Man Catch. This is a crazy idea Pansy and Helen have cooked up, by the way."

"I think it's wonderful," Pepper said, "but I didn't envision myself participating." She frowned. "So, what are we going to tell Toby and Josh?"

"About the name change?" Luke couldn't help smiling as he thought about their request. "That they've made their pop proud."

He could feel Pepper's intense scrutiny and decided his life was turning out very well—except for one piece. "The easiest thing on everyone would be if we get married," he said, "but I'm not asking you twice."

"Pretty chicken attitude for a brave bodyguard type."

"Really?"

After a moment she stopped walking and reached up to slide her arms around his neck, pulling his face down toward hers in full view of the Tulips Saloon, the jail and every other conceivable place eyeballs were probably glued to them at this moment. She kissed Luke smack on the lips and said, "I'm game for the altar if you are."

His heart beat hard inside his chest. "Do you consider that a proposal, Dr. Forrester?"

"It's the best I can do, Bodyguard McGarrett. Take it or leave it."

"I heard you were the long shot in town."

"Funny," she whispered, "that's exactly what I heard about you."

"Are we doing this for the kids?" he asked, stealing another kiss from her.

"Yes," she said. "Fighting it is getting me nowhere."

"Except on a boat in the middle of a lake," Luke teased, and Pepper shuddered. "We'll work on a better seating chart," he suggested.

"We'll work on a better *sleeping* chart," Pepper retorted, which made him grin like crazy until she added, "This is just for the sake of the children, because it's a small town and because they'll be happier."

A fake marriage? Pretending to be something he wasn't? "I accept your proposal," he said, "and the conditions."

For now. He was winning the mother of his children—he could just feel it.

He was *still* lucky.

But it was going to take more than luck to pull off keeping Pepper married—she'd turned into more of a commitment-phobe than he'd ever been. "Let's make it soon," he said. *Before you get a case of cold feet that can't be cured.*

"I'M GETTING MARRIED," Pepper told Duke and Zach the next day as they sat around the table at the ranch. Liberty and Jessica played with the kids and Molly ran around, happy to have children at the ranch. Toby and Josh, who had taken the news with delighted grins, were enjoying playing with their cousins.

"Married?" Duke said.

"Married?" Zach repeated.

"You act like you've never heard the word in this house," Pepper said defensively.

"Not said by you," Duke said. "Can we assume the lucky guy is Luke?"

"Yes." She felt good about this decision. "We're eloping this weekend."

Duke and Zach sat there quietly dumbfounded. Pepper loved the fact that she'd caught them off guard for a change.

"Eloping," Duke repeated. "The gang will not be happy."

"That's okay," Pepper said. "It's my life."

"True," Zach said, "but I warn you, they'll make you do it again if you don't satisfy their need for a full-blown wedding."

"So, where's the happy groom?" Duke demanded. "Shouldn't he be part of this wedding announcement?"

"He had a thousand chores to do with his dad," she said airily. "But he sent his regards."

Duke frowned. "Congratulations."

"Thank you." Pepper stood. "The boys are thrilled."

Pansy and Helen and Hiram and Bug and Holt would be thrilled. Bill McGarrett would be thrilled. Everyone would be happy that she and Luke had worked everything out for the sake of their sons.

She went off to join Liberty and Jessica and the children, and it struck her that she fit in, at last.

Nobody would ever know that it was just a facade, a picture of married happiness, not the real thing.

PEPPER AND LUKE GOT married at a tiny chapel in Las Vegas. It was the same one where Jessica and Zach had gotten married, because they said that would be lucky, and Luke had jumped on the idea. Pepper was so nervous she almost felt like a real bride instead of a participant in a mock wedding.

"I'm glad you talked me into this," Luke whispered as the organist readied her sheet music and the pastor cleared his throat.

"The second proposal did the trick," Pepper said.

He nodded, patting her hand. "You're a beautiful bride."

"You're a handsome groom."

Luke wished the minister—or whatever he was—would hurry up. If someone didn't say *I do* and *You're married* soon, he was pretty certain the bride next to him would disappear in a puff of bridal nerves. She was trembling, for heaven's sake, as if it was real and mattered. The moment women and men waited for all their lives—that special, magical instant when two people became one.

He was feeling pretty darn sentimental about the whole thing. Of course, he was planning on forever, so that skewed his appreciation of the ceremony. Pepper was looking for instant gratification and no sentiment. *It's the doctor in her,* he told himself. *Everything is always procedural.*

He didn't care. He was almost wed to the mother

of his children, and marriage for appearances or not, she was going to be his.

The ceremony ended after a few perfunctory "I do's." Lacking a wave of a wand and a pronouncement of happily ever after, Luke kissed the hell out of Pepper and scooped her up to carry her down the chapel steps. "Hello, Mrs. Pepper McGarrett. Dr. Pepper McGarrett, I should say."

Her lips curved with amusement. He set her down so he could kiss her again, but she pulled away faster than he liked.

"You make me sound like a soda pop," she said. "Just Pepper McGarrett will be fine."

He laughed. "You and the boys—I got all of you named McGarrett with one simple 'I do.' Pretty cool, in my opinion."

"Very efficient of you."

"Speaking of efficiency, I've rigged the Man Catch. You're sitting with me."

She smiled. "You saved me."

"The boys want to go fishing with us. We're breaking the spirit of the fish-off, but family first, I always say."

"That's one thing we agree on."

"Yes. Now, the honeymoon begins." He squinted up at the hotels surrounding them. "Can I talk you into a heart-shaped tub? They probably have those here."

Pepper shook her head. "No bathing suit."

Luke grinned. "None required."

To his surprise, his brand-new bride blushed practically strawberry. "Okay," he suggested, "let's go get some ice cream instead. Would you like that?"

"Yes," she said, losing some of the pink, and he reminded himself to slow down. The hard part was over.

They had the rest of their lives for him to lure her into heart-shaped bathtubs.

PEPPER WAS THRILLED to be married, and it wasn't just for Toby and Josh, who were ecstatic to have the family they'd always dreamed of and a father who loved them. Secretly, she had developed a craving for her husband she didn't dare admit.

She realized the craving had probably begun when he'd told the boys his name was theirs if they wanted it. When he'd made another nonserious marriage proposal, Pepper had jumped on it. When did a woman get another chance at a man who understood the needs of young boys' hearts?

She'd always been crazy about Luke McGarrett. Nothing had changed over the years, though she wouldn't have confessed that to a soul.

Luke moved into her house. Immediately, he began making changes, while she worked in her clinic. One night she came home and the boys had beds. Not just any beds, but ones with headboards and complete sets of dark brown bedding with gold cording—Ralph Lauren masculine. On the wall were framed black-and-white pictures of the boys three-wheeling with Luke.

Another night she came home and found a basketball hoop drying in cement near the driveway. Perfect for b-ball, Luke had told her. Did she want to play one-on-one with the three of them?

She couldn't figure out that math, so passed, content to spy on them from the kitchen window.

He was having a great time with the twins, and they in turn thrived under Luke's attention. A lump formed in her throat as she watched them try to outwit each other.

She didn't think she could ever get enough of watching him interact with her sons. *Our sons,* she reminded herself.

As for beds, she and Luke slept in the same one, though he never touched her. The marriage was for appearances only, as they'd agreed. For the three nights they'd been married, Pepper didn't think she'd slept a wink. She could feel Luke's heat and his strong body calling to her, and there was nothing she would have loved more than to curl up with him.

I want to make love with him.

The longing had been consuming her for days. It was beginning to obliterate the sane reasons she had agreed to the marriage. The dizzying roller-coaster ride of their relationship threatened to plunge her into sexual desire so intense she could barely think. So at night, she lay awake listening to his even breathing, imagining his bare chest rising and falling.

It was four o'clock in the morning now, and all she could do was want her husband.

"Mom," Toby whispered, from the door of the bedroom she shared with Luke.

"What is it, son?" Raising up, she peered through in the darkness.

"Josh doesn't feel well."

"All right. I'll be right there." She moved to the side of the bed and reached for her robe, shocked to feel Luke's hand close over her arm.

"Where are you going?"

"Josh is sick."

"I'll go." He got up, and before she could say anything, he left the room.

But I'm the doctor. The protest died on her lips as she realized how completely Luke intended to be a father to his children.

So she waited to be called.

"It's all right," he said, coming back into the room and sliding into bed. She glimpsed a flash of bare chest and pajama bottoms, and caught her breath. "He had a bad dream. A glass of water and some guy talk chased it away."

"What was it about?"

Luke patted the bed. "Lie down and rest. He can tell you in the morning. We didn't talk about it."

"Why not?" Pepper felt that talking about the dream would have probably helped her son.

"He just needed to go back to sleep," Luke said. "No point in reliving it and keeping him up over it. I gave him a glass of water, rubbed his back and told him to call us if he needed us."

Pepper lay in the dark, silently admiring the brisk way men dealt with their feelings. "Thank you," she murmured.

"No thanks needed," he said, sounding surprised. He rolled over to stare down at her. She could feel his heat, oh, so tantalizingly close to her. "Pepper, just because you and I have a funky marriage agreement thing going on doesn't mean I intend to short-circuit my dad duties."

"I know," she said softly.

"All right, then. Quit acting like every small thing I do for the boys is a miracle. They're mine. I love them. Relax, babe."

He rolled away and she missed his nearness immediately.

Relax.

Impossible.

Chapter Fourteen

The day of the Man Catch was beautiful, with blue skies and not-too-hot temperatures. "A perfect day for fishing," Pepper told the boys, hustling them into their swim trunks and water shoes.

"Is Luke coming?" Josh asked.

"Of course. He's changing." She left their bedroom every day when he showered and changed, too afraid of the intimacy. It would make their marriage seem real, and she didn't want to risk that.

There were too many other feelings coming to light that were risky enough. Love, for instance, Pepper thought as Luke walked out of the bedroom in blue jeans, bare feet and no shirt.

"Is there a particular dress for this occasion?" he asked. "To differentiate the caught from the uncaught males?" He grinned at Pepper. "I don't want to go in the wrong pond."

"Very funny," she said, thinking she, too, didn't want him in the wrong pond.

The boys giggled, not really understanding the

byplay but enjoying the light mood between their parents.

"Stick with us, Dad," Toby said, "we'll keep you safe."

Luke smiled. "Thanks. It's your mother's job to stake a claim on me."

Pepper stared at him. "I don't even have a good reply for that," she said, making the boys and Luke laugh.

"It is a Man Catch," Luke pointed out. "We, however, are going to catch either the biggest fish we can find or lots of little ones."

"It's going to be fun," Josh exclaimed, and Pepper went back to packing the lunch basket, completely unsettled by Luke's comment. Stake a claim on him? Was he hinting about something or was she reading too much into his teasing?

Men definitely didn't talk like that unless they wanted something, she decided, tossing in a few extra apples and a bottle of wine for her and Luke. And the only thing Luke could want was…sex.

She glanced at him when she knew he wasn't looking. Sex was a good idea, definitely one with lots of appeal. He had long, strong legs, a muscled body… *It would be great. It would be heavenly.*

But that would take their marriage to a different level. No longer could it be called a marriage for the boys' sakes. It would be for their sakes, a completely new relationship than what they'd agreed to.

The twins ran outside. Luke ambled over to inspect the picnic basket. "So, about the attire today."

She made herself look up at him, a very hard thing to do since she had a sudden attack of shyness. "I think you'll be too hot in jeans. Maybe swim trunks or shorts?"

"Are you wearing a swimsuit?" He looked at her sundress.

"I'm not planning on swimming," Pepper said. "Fishing is enough for me."

"Swimming as a family is fun," Luke countered. "I bought a couple of plastic rafts."

"You did?" She was surprised.

He nodded. "You can float while I teach the boys the joys of baiting a hook. But floating on a raft requires a bathing suit." He winked. "I'm looking forward to seeing you in one."

He made her distinctly nervous. "About staking my claim…" Pepper said, and Luke raised his brows. "I'm not sure I would know how."

"That is a problem," he murmured. "We'll have to help you work on that."

He was no help at all, she decided, and probably no help on purpose. "I think the least you could do, since I'm going to surrender to your swimsuit request, is tell me what it is exactly that you want. Or if you were just making amusing early morning chitchat."

He looked at her. "You," he said. "That's all I want."

Well, that was clear enough, Pepper thought, her heart racing deliciously. "Married a few days and regretting the terms?" she asked.

"Not regretting," he said, squatting down next to

her, "just thinking I let you go too easily." He kissed her, and Pepper knew exactly what Luke wanted her to know: the sex between them would be fantastic.

"I plan on taking very good care of you," he said a moment later, and Pepper felt herself pull back slightly from the edge she'd nearly fallen over. She shook her head.

"Luke, I'm not looking for anyone to take care of me," she said. "That's not what I want from you."

He swept her hair back over her shoulders with a smile. "I meant in bed, Miss Independent."

"Oh." She hoped she wasn't blushing as much as it felt like she was.

"Let's hit the lake," Luke said, "or I'm going to need a cold shower."

"Fishing or sex," Pepper murmured when he'd left the room. She finished packing the basket, trying to calm her suddenly trembling fingers. "I guess it all involves a hook of some kind." But she'd been thinking about sex, too, Pepper admitted. Luke was irresistible, and lying beside his nearly nude body every night was ruining her sleep.

He'd only voiced what she'd been thinking about.

Marital intimacy would make their marriage real. Right now she had the comfort of a wall of pretense. Why was she afraid of commitment? Wasn't that supposed to be a man's cop-out?

Luke had called her on it, and she knew they were facing the first real hurdle in their new life together. It wasn't that she didn't want to make love, and it wasn't that she wasn't attracted to him. *New home, new work, new marriage.*

But the changes weren't it, either. She was simply afraid of falling irreparably in love with her husband—as she had when she was a girl. She'd never really reconciled the pain of losing her first love. Having him back in her life, Pepper realized, was almost scarier than the first time. He was a natural wanderer, and though she knew he wouldn't leave this time, because of Toby and Josh, she couldn't know for certain that he wouldn't leave her heartbroken again.

She felt unformed, somehow juvenile and scarred in her ability to love. There was very little she was wary of in life, but she was afraid of falling head over heels in love with Luke and losing him once more.

Then again, he'd been talking about sex, something she'd been thinking about nonstop since they'd married.

She went to change into her swimsuit.

PEPPER HAD NEVER SEEN so many fishing boats in one place. The lake was dotted with them. "I feel like I should be helping Pansy and Helen," she told Luke. "They have to be running around like mad." The Man Catch day was certainly a success, if the number of boats were any indication.

"Valentine and some of her hairstylist friends came out from Union Junction." Luke helped Pepper into the boat, his strong hands guiding her. "Pansy and Helen specifically said you were to be a participant. I just chose to marry you before someone else could reel you in."

Toby and Josh giggled about that. Pepper smiled. "Funny, I don't feel reeled in. I feel like I caught a winner."

"Good." Luke untied the boat and pushed them away from the dock. "This is an excellent day for catching us a whopper, kids."

It felt so right, so family, Pepper thought, enjoying watching Luke steer the boat toward a place he called his "secret, giant-fish-catching hideout." Togetherness had been so easy to fall into. She watched the excited grins on the boys' faces as the boat tore across the open water. Pepper sat on the rafts to keep them from blowing out, and decided life was getting more perfect all the time.

She didn't really think Luke had a secret, giant-fish-catching hideout, but he surprised her, pulling into a cove where no other boats were present. "This is a secret?"

"Yep. Dad and I used to come here when I was young. He said he would have come today, but he didn't want to thwart the young pups in their dreams of glory."

Pepper smiled. "He looks like he's feeling a lot better."

"He is." Luke glanced at her as he secured the rafts to ropes and tossed them out. "There you go, my lady. A floating bed fit for a mermaid."

She dived over the side and hoisted herself onto one. "This is perfect. Who's the other float for?"

"Me, when the boys wear me out."

She didn't think that was likely to happen anytime soon. Luke showed the twins how to set the hooks, and for the next hour, they sat quietly. Pepper was glad of the shade in the cove.

"You know, boys," Luke said, "there used to be a granddad fish in here so big you'd hardly be able to lift him. It would take a net."

"What kind is he?" Toby asked.

"Some old lake fish that's survived countless people trying to hook him." Luke peered into the water. "He's too smart to get caught."

Pepper adjusted her sunglasses, amused by the fisherman's lore.

"Dad and I saw him once," Luke said. "He swam under our boat before we could net him. We never saw him again."

"He's probably dead by now," Josh said.

"Maybe," Luke replied. "But you never know. Some creatures can live a long time if humans leave them alone."

"Probably too old to make a good meal," Toby said, and Luke nodded.

"But we could win with it," Josh said.

"You hold your lines. I'm going to go float next to your mom. She looks lonely over there. Mermaids should never be lonely, especially one wearing a slinky red swimsuit."

He dived over the side, guaranteeing that any fish that might have been near retreated to the bottom of the lake, Pepper thought with a grin. She heard Luke clamber up on the other raft, then hers was jerked close to it. "Hi," he said.

"I heard you telling fish tales," Pepper murmured.

"I never tell tales," Luke retorted. "The truth is important."

"Boy Scout," she murmured. "Who would have guessed?" But she was glad Luke possessed a strong character and inner compass. The boys would learn a lot from him.

"I THINK DAD TOLD US about the giant grandpa fish just to keep us staring down into the water," Josh said.

"So we wouldn't watch him and Mom the whole time." Toby grinned. "We should thump their rafts."

Josh considered that. "Nah. He might get mad and go home."

Toby didn't think so. There was nothing tugging on the end of his line, and he wondered if fishing was just an excuse for adults to float and sneak a nap. "Luke's always going to be with us. He's our dad."

Josh nodded. "Mom's a lot happier now."

"Look at my bobber," Toby whispered. "It's moving!"

They sat very still, breathlessly watching. It moved again, then suddenly the line pulled so hard Toby nearly lost his fishing rod. "Dad!"

Josh tried to help him hang on to it. Toby could hear his father yelling to hold on tight, but also give the line some slack, so he tried with all his might. Whatever was pulling on it was huge!

Together the boys managed to hold on until Luke swam to the boat to help. Even his mother got in the boat to watch, and Toby was certain it was the coolest moment of his life. Having your family watch you make your first big catch was awesome.

It took them a full ten minutes to pull the fish into the boat, and when they did, they were amazed.

"It's the grandpa," Josh said in awe.

"Maybe," Luke said, "or a very near relative."

"Man, Toby, you're going to win!" Josh said.

He looked at the fish flopping around in the bottom of the boat. "Mom, quick. Please take a picture of me and Josh and our fish for Granddad."

Pepper hurriedly snapped two pictures, and Toby said, "Put him back in the water, Dad. Please."

"You don't want to win?" Luke asked.

"Naw," Toby said. "He's been down there for years. I'd rather know he's still swimming around free. Maybe one day one of my kids'll catch one of his."

Luke gently unhooked the fish, setting it carefully into the water. With a flip of its tail, the fish swam under the boat.

"Wow," Josh exclaimed, "that was crazy cool."

Toby smiled. "Thanks, Dad," he said simply. He didn't need to rob the lake of a fish to catch a man—he'd caught a dad.

That was the best prize of all.

LUKE WAS PROUD of his boys. At the end of the day, they helped him dock the boat and pack their rods into the truck. All around them giggles and laughter flowed from happy participants, and a Fish Queen and King of Tulips were crowned.

As far as he was concerned, he'd caught the most beautiful lady for himself. Or at least he was working on it, and she seemed to be slowly allowing him to romance her.

Her heart was still focused on her boys, and Luke understood he was going to have to earn his place in there with them.

He was about to load Pepper and the twins into the truck and head for home for some grilling out and maybe some wine and hopefully some romance when he heard a voice call, "Hi, Luke."

He turned to see the general and his daughters smiling at him. Beside him, he felt Pepper go perfectly still. "Hi!" he exclaimed. "What are you doing here?"

Of course he gave the girls hugs, because he'd lived with them for a year, and he shook the general's hand with genuine happiness, realizing that his old life and his new one were colliding.

"We've come to talk you into taking your old job back, Luke," the eldest daughter, Amelia, said. "We miss you!"

Chapter Fifteen

Luke glanced around. "Where are Hawk and Jelly-fish?"

The second daughter flipped her hand toward the milling crowd. "They brought us here so we could plead our case with you. But we all agree—Dad, too—that you took much better care of us."

"Oh. Thanks," Luke said, and turned to put a hand on Pepper's shoulder. "General, girls, I'd like to introduce you to my wife, Pepper. And these are my boys, Josh and Toby."

The smiles left the girls' faces. The general looked confused.

"Wife?" the youngest daughter, Sandy, said. "Luke, you haven't even been gone a month!"

"Your boys?" the middle daughter, Tonya, asked. "You mean, like, adopted?"

"I think I'll get in the truck, Luke," Pepper said softly, but he grabbed her hand so she couldn't fade away. He knew her too well.

"This is my family," he said. "So I can't come back

to work for you, although I certainly appreciate the offer. It was wonderful traveling with you all, General."

"Well," the man said, "I'm offended that I wasn't invited to the wedding, naturally, but good wishes appear to be in order. Congratulations, Luke. It couldn't happen to a nicer man. Young lady," he said, shaking Pepper's hand, "I can see Luke finally got really lucky."

A tiny smile cracked Pepper's face, and Luke relaxed. He hadn't thought she was the jealous type, but it wouldn't bother him if she showed a little wariness of other women.

"Can we invite you to our hotel for dinner?" the general asked.

"Please, Luke," one daughter said. "We want to get to know your family."

The girls looked at Pepper with pleading eyes, and he was touched when she said warmly, "We would love to come. Thank you so much for the generous invitation."

"We're only in town for a few days," the general stated. "Then it's on to the Bahamas."

"Classified?" Luke asked.

"This time, yes. We could have used you."

Luke smiled. "Hawk and Jellyfish have a good reputation."

"But they're not as good as you, Luke," one of the girls said sadly.

"Don't fret," their father said, "these honeymooners need time alone. Then maybe we can talk them into letting us borrow Luke for an odd job or two."

Luke smiled. As much as he would miss the excitement and the exotic places, Tulips held all the wonders he'd ever want to see.

The general and his girls slipped off to find a boat to join the party—ever the watercraft types, Luke thought—and he got into the truck with his family.

"That was way cool, Dad," Toby said. "I didn't know you knew a general!"

Josh leaned forward in the seat. "I really wasn't sure what to think about you being our father. But you ride three-wheelers and know how to fish and you work for a general. I like having a dad."

Luke grinned from ear to ear, feeling pretty much like a real hero.

PEPPER HAD BEEN astonished by the beautiful women who'd come to see Luke. It was hard to imagine him living with those three girls on a boat, and she would have had to be superhuman not to feel a tiny prickle of jealousy. He'd said something about being in the Greek Isles, which no doubt meant tiny bikinis and bodies that weren't stretched by pregnancy and childbirth—

"Pepper?" Luke said, as he came into their room that night.

She turned. "Yes?"

"Thank you for understanding about my former employer."

"Employers?" she teased. "It did seem the girls were the ones trying the hardest to hire you back."

He acknowledged that with a smile. "They do lead their father around, but he's stronger than he seems. He puts his foot down when they get too spoiled."

"If the general isn't careful, he's not going to get out of Tulips without a wedding ring."

"I know I didn't." Luke put his arms around her waist, and Pepper quickly decided jealousy was overrated. "I enjoyed watching you float on the raft today," he murmured. "I kept thinking you looked exactly like you do in my bed. Peaceful and calm."

He trailed small kisses along her neck. Pepper went very still, drinking in the wonder of his touch on her skin.

"The boys are in bed," Luke murmured. "You probably should be, too."

"Is that a hint?"

He slid questing hands down her arms. "If you want to consider it one."

Still no pressure. Just a gentle invitation. He was making the moment her decision.

Slowly, Pepper turned toward him, raising her lips to his. With a sharp intake of breath, Luke kissed her. It felt right, as if they'd waited a long time to get to this place.

They kissed for endless moments, discovering each other's mouths. Pepper let her hands explore the strong, winding muscles and planes of Luke's body, marveling that it felt nothing like it had when they'd made love before.

Time had ripened his body, broadening his shoulders and hardening his muscles. Pepper's pulse quickened as Luke pulled her into the bedroom they shared. He locked the door, the click a note of finality on her decision. Slowly they helped each other with clothes, but when they were naked and he'd settled her gently into their bed, Pepper knew slow wasn't what her body craved.

"Hurry," she said, kissing him urgently.

"No," he said, taking her nipple in his mouth. She moved her hands up his back, closing her eyes against the spiraling sensations overtaking her.

"Hurry," she repeated. *Before something takes you away from me.*

"It's been fourteen years," he told her, sliding a hand between her legs to tease her into anxious heat. "We don't have to rush."

She felt like rushing. She wanted his touch, and more. Magic built within her, screaming for release, and Luke kissed her when she climaxed so that she cried out against his mouth. He moved inside her and caught her gasps of pleasure again, and Pepper thought that was the best it could get—*heaven is being in bed with this man.* But then she felt more passion building, heating, tensing her body, and this time their climax was a hungry kiss they caught on each other's lips.

Perfect, Pepper thought as they lay wrapped together in the sheets. *Perfect.*

She forgot all about the general and his daughters as she basked in the glow of being Luke's wife.

PEPPER AWAKENED the next morning to Luke nuzzling her, fully ready to repeat the wonder of the previous night.

"Sun's up," he whispered against her neck.

"I get it," she said. "I'll skip the cliché reply."

He slid into her and this time the passion was raw and fast and hungry. Pepper caught her breath amid the rising tide of pleasure, shocked that he could get her body ready so fast. She cried out when she came, sending Luke to his own climax before he slumped against her. She loved to feel her power, testing his desire and arousing him to as much pleasure as she could give him. "It's so good," she said, and he nipped her neck lightly.

"It gets better from here," he said. "They say greater intimacy, greater pleasure."

She rose from the bed, pulling on her robe with a smile. "I always heard familiarity breeds contempt."

"Exactly what I would expect you to say," Luke declared giving her bottom a gentle pat as he walked by. "I intend to render that opinion as false."

The doorbell rang, startling both of them.

"Whoa," he said, "early for a visit. I'll get it."

Since she wasn't dressed, Pepper appreciated that, and watched Luke leave the room with a smile. She was more than happy to let him prove his theory of intimacy with her, over and over again.

Low voices coming from the living room made her hesitate on her way into the shower. A male visitor. Maybe Zach or Duke? But they would have called, Pepper thought. She sat on the bed to wait.

Five minutes later, Luke returned to their bedroom.

"Ah," he said, his gaze lighting on her with pleasure. "You haven't showered yet. That means I get you one more time here—" he tossed her back on the bed to strip off her silky robe "—and once in the shower. It's a twofer."

"Wait," she said, laughing, "who was at the door?"

He kissed her hard, his mouth hungry on hers, his hands roaming over her body with fierce intent. "Luke," she said, sensing he was keeping something from her, "wait a minute."

Rolling over, he pulled her on top of him so that she had the choice of a sexual encounter or not, and Pepper surrendered, sliding onto her husband with a gasp of pleasure as his hands closed over her breasts. *Intimacy,* she thought, *comes in all forms and stages.*

But something was wrong and she knew it, even as he grasped her buttocks in his hands, squeezing them so that she was tight against him. Mindless and gasping, she fell against his chest. She knew exactly the second his climax hit—only this time, it wasn't about the powerful pleasure she gave him anymore.

It was about a man trying to forget.

WHEN PEPPER AWAKENED, Luke was gone. It was nearly noon, so she jumped from the bed and called down the stairs to her boys. They had to be starving! Tossing on her robe, she hurried to the kitchen.

On the counter was a note written in Luke's strong hand:

Thought I'd let you rest. The boys and I have gone to Grandpa's for remote airplane flying. Luke

"Nice," Pepper murmured, feeling left out. At least Luke intended to be an involved father.

There was all kinds of work she could do at the clinic. She could catch up on some moving-in details around here. There were any number of things to be done; it was a matter of prioritizing, she told herself, and not getting her feelings hurt.

Her gaze caught the edge of a piece of paper sticking out from under the sofa, where it must have blown. Picking it up, she saw that it was a letter to Luke.

She would never have read anything not addressed to her, except that it was from the general. "Our early morning visitor," she murmured, her nerves tightening like stretched wire.

Luke, you're the best at what you do. I wouldn't ask if it wasn't absolutely necessary. As you know, there are benefits. I know money isn't an issue for you, but you do have a new family, and the pay is excellent. It might be worth considering this last job. It would mean a lot to me and my daughters. Your old friend, A.

Pepper's heart seemed to explode into pieces, bits of worry, shards of heartbreak. No wonder he hadn't wanted to tell her who'd been at the door. She remembered the urgency of his possession of her; she'd thought he was trying to forget something.

He'd wanted *her* to forget something, and she had. His lovemaking had swept all questions from her mind.

She had always been easy for him, Pepper realized. Always on the edge of falling in love with him. Tears welled in her eyes. "I never really got over him," she murmured.

That hurt most of all. After all these years, after trying with all her might to be her own woman, she was still crazy for the only man she'd ever loved.

Maybe he wasn't going. If he wanted to, he would have told her about the general's request. The thought comforted her, easing her past all the terrifying emotions, the dread of the unknown. She was being silly. Slipping the letter back under the sofa just as she'd found it, Pepper told herself she'd reaped her just reward for reading someone else's mail.

He would never leave the boys.

The thought should have helped. But it didn't, because she wanted to know he'd stay because of her. Yet Pepper had always known Luke was a man who didn't stay in one place.

Even though he'd promised he would.

Chapter Sixteen

Luke wanted to talk to his father about the general's proposal. In the past, he would have immediately agreed for the sake of adventure. Now he had adventure enough with a new wife and family.

"But there's some duty to consider," he told his father, who nodded.

"There's all kinds of duty," his dad said. Bill smiled as he watched his grandsons flying the remote control planes. "Family duty. Duty to country."

"I wouldn't hesitate if it wasn't the general." Luke had spent a lot of time with the man's family. In many ways, the general had been a surrogate father. The girls were the sisters he'd never had.

The part that really hung him up was that he knew the request for protection was real. The general wouldn't have asked otherwise.

"Men work," his father reminded him. "And they travel. Even ladies work and travel these days. It's nothing to get upset about. Were you planning on never working again?"

"I don't need to right now. But I do need to be a father and a husband," Luke said. "I have a lot of years to make up for."

"Guess that's your answer," Bill said.

But it wasn't and they both knew it.

"What'd Pepper say about it?"

"I didn't tell her. Yet." Had the request come before they'd made love, Luke knew he would have gone. All he and Pepper had had at that point was a marital agreement, a best-face-forward arrangement. For the boys.

Now they had a full-blown relationship as far as he was concerned. Pepper might have different ideas about that, but he intended to make sure she understood that lovemaking and intimacy were the hallmarks of a real marriage.

"You won't want secrets between you," his father advised, and Luke nodded.

"I agree. It just caught me completely by surprise."

Toby and Josh landed their planes, then inspected them carefully.

"It's our first summer together," Luke said wistfully. "I never thought I'd have kids of my own."

"They really are special boys. I sure do feel lucky." His father grinned again. "And it's not too late for more."

Luke blinked. He hadn't thought about that. He hadn't even asked Pepper if she was on the pill. Since she was a doctor, he'd assumed she would take care of birth control.

His father laughed at the expression on Luke's

face. "Wouldn't bother me a bit to have a grandbaby to hold. It'd about make my life complete."

Mine, too. But what would Pepper think about that? "Jeez," he said, feeling a grin spread across his face, "I never thought about that." He did think about getting inside her body every chance he got; he fantasized twenty times a day about hearing her cry his name with pleasure.

Oh, boy. I'm falling in love.

The unexpected knowledge thrilled him. And Pepper? She was the one who would hold back in their relationship. That would be normal, considering he'd left her before without a goodbye. She'd raised two kids on her own without involving him.

"You might think about it," his father said mildly. "I'm sure you'd like to be a more active participant this time around."

Active and involved. "This is true," Luke said. "Dad, can you watch the boys for a while? I need to talk to my wife."

His father nodded. "No need to ask twice. Leave them here for the night, if you want to. Me and the boys'll get cheeseburgers. Heck, I'll even take 'em over to the saloon and show them off to the fellows."

"And the ladies?"

"Maybe," his father said with a huge wink.

LUKE DROVE UP and parked in the garage of the house he now called home. It felt good. He'd never thought about owning a home and was surprised by how good it felt. A home, a wife, children. This was greater than anything he'd ever foreseen in his future.

Going inside the house, he felt pleasure wash over him when he saw Pepper cooking in the kitchen. "Dinner?"

She nodded. "Hope you feel like baked chicken and rice. Some steamed broccoli on the side and a chocolate cake for dessert."

"Man." He kissed the back of her neck as she stood stirring something at the stove. "How did I get so fortunate?"

"Who says you did?"

"I say so." He turned her around to kiss her tenderly on the lips. "I know I did."

She gazed up into his eyes, searching for something, he realized. "Something on your mind besides dinner?"

"No. Where are my boys?" She turned back to her cooking.

"With Dad. I think they're going to swing by the saloon later and bother Dad's new friends."

"No bother." Pepper smiled, and he wanted to touch the wisps trailing along her neck from the upswept hair she'd carelessly pulled up with a clip. "Pansy and Helen called and said they'd tried a new recipe for red velvet cake. They wanted to know if there were any takers."

"There are always takers. Did they say how the Man Catch went?"

Pepper put a lid on one pot, shaking seasonings into another. "Very well. Apparently, there were men and fish caught, and none have been thrown back yet."

"Except ours," Luke said with a proud grin.

"Yes, but that's a secret we're keeping."

She still wasn't looking his way, and Luke began to pick up some warning signs of troubled waters ahead. She was acting nonchalant and disengaged. Her posture was somewhat stiff. Whatever was going on, she wasn't going to talk about it.

He might as well head into those waters. Eventually, the honeymoon would be over, and they were going to have to discuss real life. They couldn't keep tiptoeing around everything that was uncomfortable about their lives.

"The general came by this morning," Luke began, and when Pepper turned to look at him, he figured he'd found the source of her annoyance.

"Oh?" she said softly.

"He wants me to do a little work for him." Luke glanced around for the letter he'd been given, but couldn't locate it.

"If you're looking for a letter, it blew under the sofa," Pepper said, "and I'm not proud to say I already read it."

"Ah." At least she was honest. Now he knew why she seemed troubled. "I planned to show it to you."

"Why didn't you?"

He shrugged. "I needed to take it in first. Had to think about it."

"So if you're telling me about it now you must have decided to accept."

He checked her eyes for signs of anger and saw none. Was that a good sign? "I'm considering it. Unless you object."

"No." She shook her head. "I don't."

"You don't know what I'd be agreeing to."

She nodded. "We didn't know anything we were agreeing to about each other when we got married."

That was true, but enigmatic. Luke couldn't read her and it worried him.

"I'll be very busy with the clinic. There'll be calls on the nights and weekends. I'm sure you'll find that inconvenient at times," she said. "It's sort of the nature of our respective careers."

He bit the inside of his cheek. "This isn't going to be my career, any longer. It's a last favor for a man who's been like a father to me."

She accepted that. "I married you not knowing much about you. You don't know much about me, especially regarding the years we were apart. I always thought the hardest part of dating was the beginning. People spend the first two or three dates filling each other in and catching them up about who they are, like fast-forwarding the past. It bores me."

Luke stared at Pepper. She didn't strike him as the kind of woman who liked mystery in men; he was pretty certain she was more the type who would make judicious, thoughtful decisions about the men she allowed around her sons. "Pepper, I didn't use a condom yesterday. Or today," he said.

"I know." She lifted a pot from the stove, setting

it down on a cast-iron trivet. "We didn't discuss it ahead of time."

Damn it. He couldn't ask her; he already knew the answer. She wasn't on the pill. They were heading down the same blind path as before, a pattern unbroken by the years they'd spent apart.

"I know what you're thinking," she said. "If I was worried about unprotected sex, this time I could easily get my hands on a morning-after pill."

He looked at her.

"But I wouldn't," she said. "And if you go away again, and I'm pregnant, it will be high irony, but nothing I can't survive."

There was a lot being said and a lot that wasn't, but as Luke looked at his bride, she began chopping pecans, as if they'd never said *I do.*

As if they were just two people existing inside a house.

PEPPER WENT TO THE CLINIC on Monday. She'd slept restlessly last night, but the problem was no longer frustrated sexual desire. Luke had slept on his side of the bed, as he had in the beginning of their marriage; she'd slept on hers. They never once reached for each other.

It wasn't not knowing each other, or marrying for a goal rather than love, that stole her sleep. She wanted to blame it on outside influences: the general for his request, her jealousy of his beautiful daughters—anything that might explain the sudden rift in the joy she and Luke had begun to experience.

Pansy and Helen came inside the clinic bearing cookies and a large coffeemaker. "Every good doctor's office has a couple of these machines," Pansy said, "only we're going to use this to make tea."

Pepper smiled. "And the patients who are supposed to be fasting before their blood tests?"

"They can drink it afterward," Helen said reasonably. "Take pity on your patients, Pepper. They need something to look forward to."

The ladies draped a lace cloth over a table and busily set up their treats. "Any wedding bells yet, from the Man Catch?" Pepper asked.

Helen shook her head. "But there may be some potential suitors. We'll see." She looked at Pepper. "So how is married life, anyway? Soon you'll be the authority and can counsel any new brides we might have."

"Not me," she said quickly. "I diagnose general health. Not romantic health."

Pansy nodded. "Romantic health can be hard to gauge."

Pepper didn't say anything.

"Luke's dad came into the saloon last night with the boys," Helen told her. "He mentioned that Luke might have a new job."

The Tulips grapevine was moving at its customary pace. Pepper tried to smile. "Isn't it wonderful?"

"Is it?" Pansy looked at her. "Bill didn't necessarily seem to think so."

"I don't know." Pepper picked up one of the lemon-iced cookies Pansy had laid out, not really wanting it but feeling fidgety. "We didn't discuss it much."

They gazed at her curiously. Pepper couldn't look away, because she didn't want them to think anything was wrong, but she couldn't meet their eyes, either, because something *was* wrong and it hurt. The pain was something she couldn't diagnose. "I don't exactly know what to do," she admitted.

"Can we help?" Pansy asked gently.

Pepper shook her head. "I wish you could."

They hugged her, the three of them a circle of friendship Pepper had always treasured. "I'm better with medicine than marriage, I guess."

"Well, you've heard love stinks," Helen said. "And I guess sometimes it's confusing at the very least."

"Fortunately, you have some basic material to work with," Pansy pointed out. "Luke's a good dad. He's a good husband. But there are always bound to be a few bumps."

Pepper nodded. "We agreed to marry for the children. When a marriage is built on that, maybe the foundation isn't as rock solid as it might be otherwise."

"Toby and Josh are happy," Helen said, "so obviously you made a sound decision."

That was a bright spot. "I keep telling myself it's one job. He had a life before he knew about the twins, and I do understand him wanting to finish up. Most people offer a two-week notice when they're quitting. I suppose Luke never got the chance once he returned to Tulips." It really was reasonable for him to do one last thing for the general. But Pepper couldn't help feeling as if their marriage was too new and fragile for this challenge. She knew the job must entail danger and that really bothered her—for Toby's and Josh's sake.

She took a deep breath. "As a student, I studied hard to get what I want. As a doctor, I work hard to be the best I can be. I think what bothers me most is that no matter what I do in my marriage, I'm never guaranteed of winning Luke's heart."

"Oh, dear," Pansy murmured, "I'm so sorry, Pepper."

"Uh," Helen said, "we have a tiny confession to make, too."

"What?"

"This is all our fault," she admitted. "When you came home, and we met the boys, we guessed they were Luke's. We sort of set Duke up...." She looked at Pepper, concerned and worried. "When Duke met the boys, we more or less told him whose they were, knowing full well that he'd move heaven and earth to get Luke home. And he did."

Pansy nodded. "This is the thousandth time we said we wouldn't meddle. But we always do. Now it seems it would have been better if we'd just minded our own business."

Pepper didn't think so. "So he didn't come back on his own."

They shook their heads.

"He really didn't have a chance to leave his job with the general. Basically, Duke dragged him home."

"'Drag' might be strong," Helen said, "but I doubt Luke misunderstood what was wanted of him."

"So he came home and did the right thing by me." Pepper put the Open sign in the window and a brave smile on her face. "Well, he certainly is a responsible man."

"I don't think that's exactly the way Luke sees it," Helen said. "Pepper, can you ever forgive us?"

"Oh. I'm not upset with you. Truly. I'm not even upset with Duke, or Zach or Luke, for that matter." Pepper kept the matter-of-fact tone in her voice. "It's my own fault for falling in love with Luke against my instincts. I spent thirteen years trying to forget him, and then fell for him again the first chance I got."

Pansy cleared her throat. "I'm sure he loves you, too, Pepper."

He hadn't said that he did. "Maybe." But even she didn't believe that was the case.

"Pepper," Helen said, "we have a little recipe we could share with you, if you'd like. Sometimes it helps in matters of the heart."

"I don't think a recipe could help," Pepper said. "I can cook basic meals, but that's about it."

"This is basic, too," Pansy said. "Very, very simple."

Pepper decided to humor them. "Chocolate pie? Strawberry shortcake? What will I be making?"

"Well," Helen said, "after Bill McGarrett came to see us, we cooked this up. Now, before you laugh, we'd like to say in our defense that we gave your brother Duke a recipe. We also gave Zach one, and each of their wives."

"They're just gentle words of wisdom that a mother might pass along to a daughter or son," Pansy explained. "There are no written instructions that come with marriage, you know. Success is generally about the woman and the man figuring things out. Sometimes they do and sometimes they don't."

"I'd like to figure it out," Pepper said softly.

"Luke would, too, we're certain." Pansy handed her a recipe on a pieces of paper printed with tulips. "It's all about the women being stronger than the men because they get lost in the relationship maze, the poor dears."

"Yes," Helen agreed. "We'll leave you to your patients now, but Pepper, it's all going to work out fine."

Pansy and Helen hugged her, and tears burned her eyes and the back of her throat. They departed, and Pepper looked at the recipe, if for no other reason than curiosity. She really didn't believe in the age-old wisdom that the way to a man's heart was through his stomach.

"A Recipe for Romancing Your New Husband" was written in pretty script at the top of the sheet.

Be confident! A man likes to know his wife
is happy to be married to him.

She definitely wasn't confident where Luke was concerned. Pepper sat down in her office to read more.

Focus on romance! Small surprises and lots
of laughter keep a marriage exciting. So does

Victoria's Secret lingerie and the occasional nooner. Midnight booty calls work, too, and we don't mean baby booties—although baby booties are sweet!

Pepper couldn't help laughing at their delicate attempt to coach her. Feeling better—because the recipe really was simple—she read on.

Keep precious time for just the two of you. The boys had you first, but they want you to be happy, too, which means developing a relationship that is just yours and Luke's.

They'd all been so busy getting to know each other that she and Luke really hadn't focused on the two of them as an item. It seemed wise at the time—she'd been so worried about the boys being happy—but Pepper realized Pansy and Helen were right.

She shivered, wondering if it was too late to change her ways. She'd been protecting herself from being abandoned again, protecting herself against losing Luke to the point that she never let him in, at all.

Yet secretly, she knew he wanted to go with the general, which hurt despite everything practical she tried to tell herself.

Chapter Seventeen

Luke dropped by the saloon to get Toby and Josh a snack before he went to sign them up for school. After the Man Catch, where they'd seen some kids their age, they were starting to feel excited about getting back to class.

Whether Pepper knew it or not, she and Luke had made the right decision about marrying. The boys were a lot more settled because of it.

Luke slid into a chair and grinned at Helen as she brought a menu over. "Good morning."

"I heard good news about your father, Luke," she said, as Pansy brought over drinks for the three of them to choose from.

"Yes," Luke said, "thanks to the Man Catch, Dad sold three parcels of property he owned."

"We'll have three new residents," Pansy said happily. "I can't wait to welcome them to Tulips."

"And Dad sold his business interests to Holt." Luke thought that was a smart move on his father's part. "Dad was ready to get out of residential real estate and move toward commercial. He always wanted a son to go into business with him. Holt fits the bill fine." Luke didn't feel any jealousy of Holt. It was a relief that his father wanted to stay so active now and had found a good business partner. "The boys are going to help Grandpa clean up some properties this summer, aren't you?"

They nodded eagerly, glad to be part of an enterprise that involved family.

"So, you're on your way to sign up for middle school." Helen smiled at them. "You would have liked the new elementary school your uncles built, though they about drove us crazy in the process. Tried to take our saloon for the school, but we told them women's cookies are important to a town's growth, too. Eventually, your stubborn uncles gave in."

Toby and Josh smiled. Seeing Molly at the window waving her golden tail, they dashed off to play with her.

"I'd say those are happy kids," Helen observed.

"They are."

"Your father was in here last night. He sure seems to have taken a new lease on life," Pansy said.

Luke nodded. "Amazing what grandkids can do."

Helen looked at Pansy. "I'm sure the change has something to do with a certain son being home, as well."

Luke thought about that for a few moments before deciding to make a clean sweep of it. They were going to hear sooner or later. *Might as well be from me.*

He looked at his friends. "I may be leaving for a little while."

"Oh?" Pansy said. Helen gazed at him, her eyes bright behind her black-rimmed glasses.

They must have already known because they didn't seem surprised, Luke realized. "Pepper tell you?"

"Your dad, actually," Helen said. "The boys don't know."

"I'd be back before school starts," Luke said quickly.

"We like the general," Pansy said. "How come he gets to have all the fun and excitement and derring-do?"

Luke grinned. "Because he's a general and was in command of very sensitive operations for many years."

"You must be awfully good at what *you* do," Helen said. "The general seemed very attached to you."

"I lived with his family for a year. Even though my time was spent in a protective role, we still became close. They trust me."

"So how does Pepper feel about this?" Pansy asked.

"She didn't say much," Luke said. He didn't know her well enough to know if that was a good or bad sign. Sometimes he needed two or three days to let information of a personal nature sink in.

"Guess you're looking forward to it," Helen said.

"I was in Greece when Hawk and Jellyfish encouraged me to come home," Luke said. "I never felt like I got to offer the general notice. It seemed as if I'd run out on a job and some good friends. Now they need a special favor from me, and I'd like to help."

The ladies nodded sympathetically.

"Well, of course we have no advice on this matter," Pansy said. "Thankfully, you're not looking for any."

"I am," Luke said, surprising himself. "I want to do the best thing for my family. I want to provide a good example for my boys."

Pansy smiled. "People in the military spend time away from their families. Pilots have to travel. Lots of people travel for work. Talk it over with Pepper. And then I'm sure your feelings will guide you to the best decision."

He wasn't so sure. He felt completely divided. The right thing to do would be to finish up with the general and be proud of a job well done before he moved on with his life. On the other hand, his marriage was quite new, his bonds with his boys just forming.

The timing felt awkward, but then, the timing had felt awkward in many ways since he'd been in Tulips.

He wouldn't be feeling split if he hadn't seduced Pepper. Once he'd known the wonders of being with her, his priorities had begun to change.

Not to mention that the sex was mind-blowing.

"Luke?" Helen said. "Are you all right?"

"I'm fine." He sat straighter and tried to focus. It was weird what Pepper was doing to his brain.

Pansy poured him some tea. "Blackberry," she said helpfully. "You look like you could use a cinnamon cookie, too."

It wouldn't help. His face would still go slack, his

eyes dreamy, if he was thinking about Pepper, which was all he did anymore. A trip with the general would give him perspective, Luke decided. He was in danger of making a major goof in his life. Pepper hadn't wanted a heavy-duty marriage tying her down. They'd agreed to marry for the boys' sake, but he'd been unable to resist making love to her.

Definitely not in the spirit of their agreement, which again was all his fault. Where Pepper was concerned, he was no different than he'd been at seventeen. *Horny.*

"Marriage isn't easy for me," Luke said suddenly. "I know what to do with guns. I can travel all over the world without suffering from jet lag or Montezuma's revenge. Nothing bothers me. Except marriage," he confessed. "I can't quite get the woman's angle down."

"Lots of romance helps," Helen advised.

And Pansy added, "Lots of kissing and hugging and bedtime fun."

Luke blinked, staring at his friends. "Check, check and check."

A concerned frown settled on Pansy's brow. "Well, all that's left is good communication."

He felt that he and Pepper communicated well. But they did operate differently. "She didn't really want to marry me," he said. "I coerced her. I figured women secretly want to be married, and I could make her happy and we belonged together because of the boys—"

"Oh," Helen said, "this is a falling-in-love problem."

Luke wasn't sure what it was, but he was willing to accept some words of wisdom. "Can it be solved?"

"Maybe," Pansy said. "We have a recipe you can try. We make no guarantees, though."

"A recipe? I let Pepper cook if she feels like it. And then I do KP. Kitchen police," he explained.

"Well, at least you do something," Helen said, rooting around in a drawer. "I think Bug and Hiram started out doing nothing. Most men are like that, until their wives stop cooking to make their point! Here it is," she said, pulling out a piece of paper and handing it to Luke.

"'A Recipe For Winning Your Independent Wife,'" he read aloud. "Obviously, you must have known I might bobble my marriage slightly."

"No," Helen said, "but Duke and Zach each got a recipe awhile back, so we made one up for you, too. We didn't want to seem preferential."

"It's just that there is no foolproof guidebook for marriage," Pansy explained.

"The unknown can be a bit scary," Helen said. "But between us, Pansy and I were married many years. We decided marriage really was a simple recipe, perhaps more simple than any we cook up in our kitchen. It's the recipe people are lacking."

"Maybe." Luke folded the paper and put it in his pocket. "Thanks for trying to help."

They smiled. "Luke, you've turned out real well," Helen said.

"If you think about it, you've done the hard part

in your life." Pansy said. "You've made your father a happy man."

He and his dad had come a long way, Luke acknowledged. Reconciliation was something he'd learned to appreciate.

"I think it's somewhat fun that we split the great debate of commerce versus organic growth," Helen said, a twinkle in her eye. "Duke got his organic growth, all courtesy of the Forresters, I might add. Three new families. And the Tulips Saloon Gang—"

"Proponents of commerce to build Tulips," Pansy interjected.

"—also added three families." Helen could barely contain her glee. "Good things are happening all over our fair town. And you and your family looked really happy at the Man Catch. It did us good to see it."

Kissing them both goodbye, Luke left and went home, thinking about his own contribution to Tulips's organic growth. He and Pepper had a lot to discuss.

As he parked the truck outside the house, he saw his sons and a golden retriever disappear inside. Luke wondered how Pepper would feel about a dog roaming through her place. Since it was Duke's dog—and probably partly hers and Zach's, as well— he figured she wouldn't mind too much. He'd know soon enough if the dog swiftly exited.

Idly, he pulled out the paper the ladies had given him. There wasn't anything they could tell him about marriage that he wasn't well on his way to messing up, he decided.

He wasn't too proud to admit he could use some well-meaning tips. With some trepidation, he gazed at the first ingredient.

Real men communicate. Really, they do.

There was a lot he couldn't talk about, though. The general's work had classified status; even wives weren't privy to that information. The general's real issue of concern was his daughters. While he felt safe with Hawk and Jellyfish, he wanted one more pair of eyes—Luke's eyes—watching out for his girls. Kidnapping had been a real fear of his; ransom and terrorism seemed to go hand in hand. Now that Luke had sons of his own, he understood the general's concern.

But he couldn't explain a lot of this to Pepper. Some, yes. All, no. He couldn't discuss it with anyone.

Nor could he tell her that it felt like he'd run out on family. He had so much family *here* now. Plus, it was true what he'd told Pansy and Helen: he had sweet-talked Pepper into marrying him. She hadn't been particularly keen, especially since she'd been surviving well enough on her own, raising the boys.

Luke felt torn. The job was short, only a couple of months, just long enough to accompany the general and his family to South America. He'd be back before the boys were in school.

His gaze drifted to the second ingredient.

Remember romance. Old movies, alone time, flowers from the garden, walking under the stars on a cold night.

He hadn't romanced Pepper much. Would she want that? From what he knew, she was a woman who didn't like a lot of frills. Just straight answers and a professional approach. The doctor preferred information she could readily process.

He'd sure give it a whirl if the ladies thought it was a good idea, though.

Give yourself a chance to learn. No one has all the answers for marriage, at first. The first year is all learning curve.

He needed his curve to be a quick one.

Putting the letter away so he could think over the advice, he went inside the house. Toby and Josh and Molly were on the sofa, watching cartoons. The dog gave him a sheepish glance, and the boys barely nodded when he ruffled their hair.

"No dogs on the sofa," he said, feeling a little bit like the bad guy. "Down, Molly."

She slunk to the floor, lying down at the boys' feet.

"You knew better than that, you old ham." Luke went upstairs to find Pepper.

He discovered her up on a ladder in the hall, pulling wallpaper off one corner of the wall. "Need help?"

She gazed down at him with some surprise. "Have you ever done this before?"

"I hate to admit it, but no."

She smiled. "Then I'll pass on making you strip wallpaper."

He thought about the gang's recipe and considered the best way to open up some communication. "I could make dinner," he suggested.

That got her attention. She stared at him. "Really?"

"Of course," he said, making it sound as if he were Julia Child and knew what he was doing. "If you eat grilled, I can grill it."

"I love grilled food." She went back to her work. "I warn you that there are no groceries, though."

"I'll sign on for shopping, too. Or," he said, thinking about romance, "we could order pizza and then take a long walk together. I could teach you how to find Orion's belt."

She laughed. "This is Tulips. We don't get pizza delivery here. We don't have any delivery, unless you count Valentine, who kindly brings confectionary items to the saloon."

"So," Luke said, "are we okay with each other?"

"I think so," Pepper replied, but she didn't seem surprised that the question came up.

"Could we be better?"

She tore off another strip of wallpaper. "I don't honestly know."

He thought about that. "You'd tell me if you weren't good with me doing this last job?"

She was silent for at least half a minute. "Luke,

you had a life before us. I didn't expect you to give up everything for us."

Did that sound odd? Something didn't ring sincerely, as reasonable as she made it sound. He watched her strip a few more pieces, realizing he'd gotten all the answer on that subject she intended to give.

"I'll grill chicken," he said, and she nodded.

"Thank you."

Thank you for cooking dinner? He desperately wanted to snatch Helen's and Pansy's words of wisdom from his pocket—he needed a cheat sheet. *Romance,* he reminded himself. "You've got a great butt in those jeans," he said. "You could stand on a ladder like that all the time so I could stare at it. But then I'd miss out seeing your…face," he said, hesitating only long enough so she'd think he'd been about to say *breasts.*

She looked down and giggled, finally making eye contact, to his great satisfaction. "Maybe I will let you show me Orion's belt tonight," she said.

The recipe was working.

He sure hoped it was, because if it wasn't, he was running out of ideas on how to convince his new bride that their marriage was about more than Parenting 101.

Chapter Eighteen

"So what I was thinking," Luke said to Pepper when she joined him in the kitchen thirty minutes later, "is that it still feels like we're dating, as opposed to married."

She hesitated, thinking about the recipe she'd studied as hard as any medical journal. "We've had a lot to absorb in the few weeks we've been married."

"True."

He touched the back of her neck as she pretended interest in the dinner he was preparing. She didn't think she could eat. New bride nerves, she told herself. Marriage wasn't easy, despite the gang's help. "When do you leave?"

"Tomorrow."

Her heart fell, dropping a thousand feet to nowhere. Shocked, she turned to face him, and he moved his hand away. "So soon?"

He nodded. "The general is in Dallas. I'll go with them, as will Hawk and Jellyfish."

She sank into a kitchen chair. "I don't think I completely understand exactly what it is you do."

"I was in the military for a few years. After high school, when I left here, I did a lot of rolling around. A bit of cowboying, joined the rodeo for a while. I was lucky a lot. What I wasn't was responsible. I joined the military to have a connection."

"I didn't know that," she murmured.

"My father knows. We argued bitterly about it." He shrugged. "That doesn't matter anymore. But at the time, it hurt."

"I'm sorry," she murmured.

"Dad always felt that I had an incredibly lucky streak that would one day run out. I did have a lot of good fortune, but a lot of it I made on my own. You don't cowboy and win unless you work hard. You don't make good real estate investments unless you study the market—it's not luck. I worked hard in the military, and when I got out, I had the respect of my superiors, in particular, the general. I've stayed with him in a protective capacity, thanks to the skills I acquired."

"It sounds dangerous." Her heart sank.

"I like to think of my life as well-rounded." Luke pulled her toward him, though Pepper tried to shrink away. She'd married him without knowing very much more about him than the boy she'd remembered. Now she knew his world—his job—was inherently dangerous, and she wanted to put her head down and cry.

"It was well-rounded until I married you and became a husband and a father," he said simply. "Now I feel complete."

She looked at him. "You aren't complete, yet."

"No?" Releasing her hand, he studied her.

"We don't have a marriage," she said softly. "We're married, but we don't have a *marriage*. Not yet." She turned away. "I guess there will be time for that when you return."

"I'm sorry, Pepper." He stood behind her, holding her arms. "You and the boys…you're my world now. But I need to finish some things in my old world."

"I understand. I even admire it." She took a deep breath. "But that doesn't mean I have to like it."

He turned her toward him and kissed her so deeply, so sweetly, that Pepper reached over with one hand, flipped off the oven and walked her husband to their bedroom.

They had no time to lose.

LUKE WALKED INTO his sons' bedroom at four o'clock that morning. The hardest thing in the world was leaving these people. No wonder soldiers joked that if the military wanted you to have a wife, they'd issue you one. This new family he'd been blessed with made it very hard to go. He touched Josh's hair while he slept and then Toby's.

Toby sat up, rubbing his eyes. "Hey, Dad."

Josh sat up, too. "Is it morning?"

"It's morning," Luke said, "but not time to get up. I didn't mean to wake you." Secretly, he was glad they'd awakened. He'd get one last hug goodbye from his boys.

"Are you going?" Toby asked.

"Yeah." He hugged his sons. "I'll be back before school starts."

"Promise?" Josh demanded. "Remember, you married Mom so that we'd have your name in time for school. But a name isn't much unless your dad drives you to school on the first day."

Luke smiled. "I didn't marry your mom just for that," he said. "Well, I did, I guess, but that's not why I'm married to her now."

Toby sank back against the covers. "We know why you're married to her now," he said, yawning.

Luke hesitated, thinking about the passionate encounter he and Pepper had just shared. Very, *very* passionate. "Oh?"

"You like us," Josh said.

"Yes, I do." Luke kissed his boys' foreheads and rose. "Let your mom sleep in if she wants, okay?"

"Sure, Dad," they said sleepily.

"I'll be back soon," Luke told them, his eyes burning with tears he was glad they couldn't see. "I love you both very much."

"We love you, too."

They rolled back over and he slipped out, telling himself he'd accomplished at least one goal: he had a good relationship with his sons, something he'd wanted all his life with his own father.

First day of school: September 1. It was a date he had etched in his mind.

KNOWING LUKE WAS LEAVING, and waking up to find him gone and a rose on the pillow beside her, were two completely different things. Her heart sank even as she took in the romantic gesture. Unable to help herself, she allowed herself a brief moment of tears and some panic. She'd fallen in love with her husband, something she'd never expected—not this type of love. That teenage crush she'd harbored had slowly ripened into a wonderfully delicious love of which she'd only dreamed.

He was right, though, about the separation between them. She'd kept herself aloof mentally, always afraid of being left again.

And now she was. Only this time it was different, she reassured herself. He'd said goodbye. She knew where and why he'd gone.

He's coming back. He loves his boys.

He'd developed a great relationship with his father. Luke would return for that reason, too.

She got up and dressed, though it was six o'clock in the morning. Patients would arrive at the office around eight-thirty, for which she was thankful. Her work would keep her busy, as it always had.

Realization struck her. If Luke hadn't left Tulips back then, she might not have become a doctor. *I probably would have never left Tulips, like so many other girls here. I would have stayed, waiting around for Luke to marry me. But we were far too young....*

Her education had become her priority. She had a family to raise, and that had given her a mission.

It had all worked out. She knew that now—she'd been just as lucky as Luke.

When he comes back, I'm going to tell him that I

love him. I'm not losing any more precious days
without telling my husband that he's been the love
of my life.

TWO WEEKS LATER, Pepper woke up nauseated. She'd
fixed eggs and bacon for herself and the boys last
night after she'd picked them up from the Triple F,
where they spent their days while she worked. If
they weren't at the ranch, they were with Luke's
father. This arrangement suited everyone: Duke
and Zach felt that they were getting to spend time
with their nephews and Bill had a ton of projects he
couldn't wait to do with the boys. Pepper had never
seen such a fast turnaround in someone's life as she
had in Bill's. He literally thrived, spending time with
his grandsons.

I'm not thriving at this moment. She went into the
bathroom, uneasy with nerves, but couldn't shake the
nausea. Wondering if the boys were feeling ill, too,
she went to check on them. They slept soundly, worn
out from the days' activities. Molly slept at the foot
of their beds, a new habit the golden retriever had acquired. It was a short walk for the dog from the jail,
where Duke worked, and every day, when the boys
got home, Molly was waiting on the porch. Sometimes, when Duke picked the boys up to go to the
ranch, Molly hitched a ride out with them and
returned at the end of the day. She always seemed to
know which days Duke was at the jail and which he
spent with the twins, and adjusted her routine accord-
ingly.

The boys were thrilled. They'd never had a dog.

Backing out of their bedroom, Pepper closed the door. The nausea had passed slightly, but she went to the kitchen and grabbed a ginger ale. It was then she noticed her breasts felt slightly tender. With her heart beating a bit more rapidly, she checked the calendar on the kitchen wall.

She was four days late, despite being normally regular. *Stress,* Pepper told herself, but the sinking feeling inside told her something completely different.

Two hours later, after the boys and Molly left with Duke, Pepper hurried to her clinic. She pulled out a pregnancy test she had on hand for patients, telling herself she was making herself crazy for no reason.

The thin blue line that immediately popped up on the test told a different story. Breathless, Pepper sank into a chair.

I'm so happy. I'm so scared!

History was repeating itself. Once again, Luke was gone—and once again, she was pregnant.

Disbelief washed over her before delight took hold. This time, she was married. This time they would share the joys of pregnancy.

Not share. It wasn't as if she could call him, and even if she could, she wasn't sure she would. She didn't want him worrying about her.

Of course, not telling him about her previous pregnancy had put a dent in his trust of her. The omission had started their marriage at a deficit. The one thing he'd asked of her was not to keep things from him anymore.

But this… She couldn't tell him. Not now.

Anything could happen.

She wanted his mind on his job. It was his last one, he'd said, of the bodyguard variety.

Then he'd be all hers, and the boys' and the new baby's. They'd start over as a family.

This time, it would all work out.

The doctor in her noted her rapid pulse and flushed skin. All the years of worry and struggle, when she'd faced raising children alone, rose to taunt her.

It would all work out. It had to.

Luke was a man of his word.

Chapter Nineteen

Pepper kept her news to herself for another two weeks. Though her body was giving her clues, she wanted confirmation that she wasn't imagining her pregnancy.

She took another pregnancy test, which only confirmed that she hadn't dreamed the baby into existence.

Dreaming it wasn't so far-fetched. Over the two weeks she'd given herself to take in everything that had happened between her and Luke, she'd realized she wanted more children. Now that she was married to the father of her twins, having another child had become a fantasy for their future together.

She hadn't expected the fantasy this soon. Yet her surprise turned to joy, tinged only by regret at Luke's absence.

The one dilemma was that she couldn't share the good news with him, she thought wistfully. Pepper prayed he would come home safely so they could share the magic of pregnancy together.

She didn't want to think what she would do if he didn't—couldn't—come home for the first day of the boys' school, as he'd planned. The possibility was enough to wake her up in the middle of the night.

He'd said he would call her when they got to certain areas he would deem safe. *I can tell him when he calls,* she assured herself, staring anxiously up at the ceiling. And she then realized in the next thundering heartbeat that she couldn't. She didn't want his attention diverted from the job he wanted to finish.

But was she making the correct decision this time? He'd been very angry when he learned she'd never told him about the twins.

"This time I'll still be pregnant when he comes home," she told his father as they sat outside his house, watching the boys play with the radio-controlled planes Luke had given them. "It's a different situation this time."

Bill scratched his head, pondering that. "It is different. I don't know how to change it. Still, I'm sure he'd want to know."

They sat quietly in the gathering twilight. Pepper had decided it was wise to tell the person closest to Luke, who knew him best—despite their years of bitterness—about the expected addition to the McGarrett clan. "It's only a couple of months," she murmured. "I don't want to jeopardize anything he's doing."

"I know." Bill thought about that. "Even if we sent a message, I don't know that it would get through."

"That's true."

"Do the boys know?"

She shook her head. "I've told no one except you. You're Luke's closest relation. I could tell the twins, but I feel like he should be with me when we tell them." The whole thing was out of order, and not the way she'd dreamed their future would unfold. "It's too soon."

"Don't say that, gal. Everything happens for a reason. I, for one, am delighted to have another grandchild on the way. Bet this one's a girl," he said happily. "I can just feel it."

She smiled. "Toby and Josh would love a little sister. But they'd love a little brother, just as well." Pepper herself couldn't help dreaming of pink onesies, pink blankets, a white crib with lots of lace and frills.

"Luke's going to be the happiest man on the planet," his father said. "I can't help you with advice about when to tell him, though. He'd want to come home if he knew you were pregnant, but he wouldn't leave this assignment. It's highly classified," Bill admitted.

"Dangerous?" Her heart started slowly sinking at the ominous words. Luke had made it sound like he was just doing a favor for an old friend and employer.

"We won't think about those things, Pepper," Bill said softly. "We'll think about how wonderful it is to be expecting a baby."

She shook her head, her physician's soul weighing the information she was receiving.

"You might go ahead and tell the gang," Bill suggested. "You'd have the ladies to help you this time."

Pepper nodded, but the truth was beginning to hit her. Luke might not come back for a long, long time. She'd never felt so helpless in her life and the worst part was that she hadn't once told him she loved him. Insecurity had kept her silent.

It was a bitter lesson to learn.

PANSY AND HELEN SQUEALED with joy when Pepper told them about the baby.

"This is wonderful news!" Pansy said. "I bet Luke is thrilled!"

"I haven't told him," Pepper admitted, "but I have told his father."

"You haven't heard from Luke?" Helen asked.

"No." She tried to make her reply breezy, as if she was doing fine in spite of the lack of communication. "But I called Aunt Jerry, and she's ready to move down here. She says she misses us and she won't miss the cold at all. The boys are so excited—that news just about makes their world perfect. Holt says he's got the perfect house close by us for Aunt Jerry. It couldn't be more perfect."

The chatty front was getting on her nerves, but Pepper didn't know what else to do but put on a brave face.

Helen and Pansy looked at her with some dismay. "So you didn't really have time to put the recipe to work," Helen said.

Pepper shook her head, feeling that lack poignantly. "When Luke comes home, we'll have plenty of time to become close." Her statement sounded so empty and worried that she smiled to cover that fact. "I'm taking up knitting."

"Knitting?" Pansy's lips quivered as if she might cry. "Booties?"

"Wouldn't that be nice?" Pepper said brightly. "When I get beyond the basics, that is."

The ladies looked worried. "Well," Helen said, "men are mysterious beings. That's all I know, I guess."

"We never knew much," Pansy admitted, "we just tried to act like we did in case it helped. Guess we didn't help you as much as we wanted to."

"Maybe it all started badly. Maybe my mistake was beginning my marriage with a lie." Pepper shook her head. "My bigger mistake was not being honest when I had the chance. Falling in love with Luke scared me so much. I kept thinking that if I was scared, something must be wrong. The only thing that was wrong was me, I suppose."

Helen shook her head. "If perfect relationships exist, I sure don't know about them. Marriage is about forgiving the small things. I'm certain Luke had forgiven you, Pepper."

"And I know he loves you," Pansy declared.

The thought cheered Pepper immensely. "I hope so," she murmured. "When I think about the dreams I've had in my life, Luke loving me would certainly be one come true."

Something was nagging at her, though, a worry she couldn't quite pin down. "I feel as though history is repeating itself and that I'm making the same mistake again. It's not practical, but I feel like I should at least make the effort to get word to Luke about the baby." Pepper had thought this through a hundred times, and each time, common sense told her it was best to tell him when he returned.

But her heart told her that Luke would want to know about the baby as soon as possible. "So he'd know I really want him in my life," she murmured, and the ladies perked up.

"You do, don't you, Pepper?" Pansy asked.

"I do. So much that it hurts. I held back because of trust issues, but I needed to learn to trust myself the most." Pepper took a deep breath and gazed at her friends. "I'll figure this out. I'll make the right decision."

"Like you always have," Pansy said supportively. Helen nodded, patting Pepper's arm.

Pepper smiled, feeling their love and their belief in her. No matter what, she was going to make her marriage work.

And yet despite her best efforts, Pepper knew she wouldn't tell Luke. She was afraid of endangering his mission, that was true, but a deep, troubled part of her wanted to know that he would actually come home to her. Not just because of Josh and Toby, but come home to her and the marriage they hadn't really started off with romance and hopes of fairy tale, happy endings.

ON AUGUST 31, after Pepper had laid out Toby and Josh's new school clothes and school supplies for the next day, she faced the fact that she had to tell her sons their father wouldn't be home in time for their first day of school. She hadn't heard from Luke, and neither had his father. It was as if he'd disappeared off the face of the earth. The boys' hearts would be broken, and she didn't know what to say to them to make it better, except that their dad would be here if he could.

Pepper was beginning to show. She'd finally sat down and told the boys, realizing she had to do it before they found out at school, from friends who'd overheard their well-meaning mothers talking. Though Pepper wore dresses to minimize her condition, this time she'd started showing a lot earlier.

Toby and Josh were ecstatic. They wanted the baby to arrive in time for Christmas. Pepper had told them the newborn would most likely be born in March, which had taken some of the edge off their excitement.

They were tired of waiting for everything, Toby complained, and Pepper knew he meant his father's promised return home for the first day of school.

She didn't let herself think about how, when Luke saw her again, she'd seem awfully out of shape compared to the tiny blondes in bikinis he'd been guarding. *I just want him home safe. Healthy. Mine.*

God, she just wanted him home with her, so she could touch him and hold him. So they could play with the boys, and visit with Bill and let Molly break the rules about dogs on the sofa.

"Mom?" Toby said, coming into the kitchen, where she sat staring into a cup of herbal tea. "Have you heard from Dad?"

She put on a brave face for the boys. "Not yet."

Josh sat down and stared at her. "Mom, he's not coming back."

Chills ran through her. "What makes you say that?"

"He's just not," Toby said with certainty. "We asked Grandpa where Dad was, and even he doesn't know. It's just like before. We might as well have never known we had a father."

Tears pressed at her eyes but she refused to give in to the same worry. Right now, her boys needed to feel her strength. "I believe he's coming," she said steadfastly, her voice firm. "I'm never going to believe anything else."

"There's about twelve hours until school starts. He's not coming," Josh said, and for the first time, she heard a note of despair in his young voice.

"He will if he can."

Toby and Josh looked at her, their spirits low. She didn't know what to say to make it better, and she had doubts of her own, so she tucked the boys in bed, sitting in their room until they fell asleep.

Outside the window, she could see the moon rising high in the sky, like a guiding light. *He would have come back if he'd wanted to,* Pepper thought, and suddenly, she realized she couldn't be married for the sake of the children anymore.

An absent husband did not a marriage make, especially a marriage that had been planned from the beginning to be in name only.

Chapter Twenty

On the morning of the first day of school, Pepper quietly got in the van with her sons. She thought perhaps they were slightly embarrassed that she was showing and even more upset that their father wasn't around to be with them. They'd really wanted Luke at their side so that all the kids would see that the new boys had a family, a real family.

Pepper blinked back tears. She didn't know what to say to her children. Her family had been a close one, so she could sympathize with their feelings.

At the middle school, they got out and walked inside. Pepper tried to hang back a bit in order not to embarrass her boys, who were getting a few interested looks from girls. They were too nervous to notice as they searched for their classroom. With one last anxious glance over their shoulders at Pepper, they looked at each other, completely oblivious to the kids filing in past them.

Go on, she wanted to say. *Walk through that door.*

Once you open the proverbial closet doors, you'll see that there was never a monster inside.

"Toby and Josh?" she heard a man say, and they nodded, staring up at a teacher Pepper didn't recognize. She'd been gone a long time and no longer knew everyone in Tulips. But he gazed at her boys with a kindly smile, glancing over to where she hovered in the hall.

"Dr. McGarrett?" he said, and she nodded, forcing a smile.

"I'm Bart Grady, world history teacher."

She shook his hand. "Nice to meet you."

His eyes twinkled. "Please come in with Toby and Josh."

"Oh, I shouldn't." She edged back slightly, not wanting the other kids to think Toby and Josh needed their mother to make everything okay for them.

"You should," Bart said. "There's a surprise for you three, I believe."

With great trepidation, she walked into the classroom, a room she hadn't been in in fourteen years. In front of the chalkboard, on the teacher's pedestal chair, sat Luke, unshaven and wild-haired and wearing a grin. She stared at him.

"Guest lecturer for world history," he said, and the boys flew into his arms. Tears of joy jumped into Pepper's eyes. He smiled at her over their sons' heads. "And I have souvenirs for the whole class," he said. "South American chocolate."

His gift made Luke an instant hero. Pepper wiped a few tears away and retreated into the hall, certain that they'd disrupted Mr. Grady's class enough. But the delight on her boys' faces was something she'd remember for the rest of her life.

"I'll call roll," Mr. Grady said, "and then we'll enjoy the honor of Mr. McGarrett starting our year off with a bang—introducing history from the perspective of someone who's recently traveled the world. And maybe if you all are very, very lucky, one day you'll be able to travel to exciting countries, as well."

Pepper slipped away. So many emotions ran through her that she felt she had to escape before she totally embarrassed her boys and gave in to the hormone-induced tears she was going to cry at any second. Happiness, excitement, surprise—they were all mixed in there, from just one thought.

Luke had kept his word to his sons.

He was certainly their hero.

PEPPER WAS SITTING at her desk around noon when Luke came into her office. She stayed seated so he wouldn't see her stomach. There was a lot she wanted to know before she revealed her secret.

"You left," he said.

"I did? Or was that you?" she replied.

He perched on her desk. "It doesn't matter. I'm back now. Are you?"

She looked at him, hiding all the gratitude she felt at his safe return. All morning she'd been a bundle of nerves. "Is it that easy? You were gone longer than we were married."

He looked at her.

"Let's start with an easier question," she hedged. "Was the operation a success?"

"Yes."

"You look well."

"The airports were harder to get through than the assignment," Luke said. "I darn near didn't make it in time for the first day of school."

Pepper noted the dark circles under his eyes. "Your arrival was better than Santa Claus," she said. "I feel certain the boys' apprehension about starting a new school is completely gone."

"I left the class debating whether they would prefer South America or Greece for their first travel adventure," he said with a grin. "Mr. Grady seemed to have the discussion well in hand. And I met the boys' other teachers."

"You did?" Pepper hadn't met any besides Bart Grady.

"Of course. I signed up for library duty once a week. And maybe some assistant coaching, if the boys don't mind me helping with the soccer team."

"Soccer team? Does Tulips have one?"

He laughed. "This one will have to be coed so we'll have enough players, but the idea went over very well. I think it will all work out."

"Liberty could design uniforms," she murmured.

Luke touched Pepper's chin, turning her to face him. "Glad to see me?"

"Of course." She swallowed, trying not to burst into tears at the question. "How could I not be?"

"With you, I'm never sure."

She took a deep breath. "About that. I missed you, Luke. Very much."

He smiled, pleased. "Dragged from the depths of your soul?"

"No." She shook her head. "I'm not trying to make you guess at what I think. From now on, you'll know how I feel about you. About us. If that's what you want."

"I do." He looked at her a long time. "I missed you like hell."

She blinked. "Thank you."

He laughed. "So formal."

"I don't know what else to say," she said helplessly. "I'm afraid you're not back…that you didn't come back because of me. Just for the boys."

He shook his head at her. "Pepper, you are such a doubting lady. So many mysteries and secrets. But I have a lifetime to wring all those doubts right out of your overly intelligent brain. You just think too much, and it's usually about all the scary stuff."

"I'm always telling the boys that everything will work out all right," Pepper murmured, and he nodded.

"Just like this. No more starting and stopping. It'll be easier now that I'm home for good."

She lowered her gaze, afraid to believe him. "Luke," she said softly, "this is going to be anticlimactic for you, after traveling around the world on secret missions and watching beautiful women in clandestine locations, but we're having another baby."

He laughed out loud. "You are such a doubter."

Getting up, he locked the office door and jumped over her desk so that he could pull her to him. His hands spread over her stomach, searching for signs of her pregnancy. Pleasure flared in his dark eyes. "So you were keeping one last secret," he said with a smile. "I'm going to have to keep a very close eye on you, Dr. McGarrett."

She smiled as he kissed her tenderly on the mouth. "I'll let you, Bodyguard McGarrett," she said when he looked down into her eyes. "And one last thing. I love you, Luke. I don't think I ever got over you, and you can call that information 'unclassified.' Clear enough on the feelings issue?"

"I'm a man who appreciates unclassified these days. Damn sexy of you to be pregnant when I get home," Luke said, letting his hands roam over her waist.

"I like to think I one-upped you on the cool souvenirs."

"Yeah, I have to say a baby beats South American chocolate," Luke said, pulling her toward him again. "I'm the luckiest man alive."

"Not yet," Pepper said with a secretive smile, "but how about a nooner, husband?"

He grinned and slid her onto the desk. "Lucky, lucky me."

Epilogue

The baby came early the next year, on Valentine's Day, which Luke thought was very romantic of her. His radiant wife held his new daughter—whom they named Helen Pansy McGarrett and nicknamed Ellen for the sake of clarity—and Luke was certain he'd never seen Pepper more beautiful.

Aunt Jerry was at home, helping the boys do their homework, though Luke suspected very little was getting done, since they knew their little sister was on the way.

Ellen snuggled against her mother, and Luke grinned. "I'm not missing a thing this time. Not the diapers, not the breast-feeding, not the spitting up. I'm going to enjoy every minute of this."

Pepper smiled at him. "It feels as though we're starting everything over."

"I was thinking it was like we had the old, and we've got the new and it's all just right." Luke handed Pepper a small box. "Something for the just-right doctor in my life."

Holding his gaze with hers, Pepper took the box. Slowly, she opened it, finding a beautiful diamond ring inside.

"Marry me again, Pepper," Luke said, "here with all our friends and family."

She nodded, and he thought he saw tears of happiness in her eyes. "Did the gang put you up to getting married in Tulips? Zach said they would want us to be formally married, meaning they get to be in on everything."

He shook his head. "They never said a word about it. This is all my idea."

"Really?" That meant more to her than she could ever say. "Think they gave up meddling?"

"I hope not," he said, kissing her as he slipped the ring on her finger. "I sure hope not. We've got a bunch of little Forresters and McGarretts depending on them and their recipes of love."

"IT WAS WONDERFUL how it all worked out, wasn't it?" Pansy said to Helen as they locked the door of the saloon. "So romantic."

"For all the Forrester kids." Helen smiled as she looked at the stained glass door. The sight never failed to bring her pleasure. "I'm glad Pepper got a door to match this one for her clinic. It gives Tulips such a connected look."

Pansy allowed Helen to take her arm as they companionably walked down the sidewalk. Bug and Hiram fell into step with them when the two women reached Duke's jail.

"What's up, ladies?" Bug asked.

"Just reminiscing," Helen said. "We were talking about how wonderful everything turned out."

"Yeah," Hiram said. "Duke said that after we throw the wedding for Pepper and Luke, we're all taking turns watching Toby and Josh."

"Oh?" Pansy said. "Something romantic afoot?"

"Luke said something about wanting to get Pepper into a heart-shaped bathtub," Bug said, and Helen grinned.

"Good recipe work," Pansy told her.

And Helen replied, "Same to you."

"Although we can't take credit," Pansy said, as the four of them walked toward Helen's and Pansy's houses. As Duke walked out of the jail for the night with Molly at his side, she called, "Howdy, Sheriff."

"Howdy," he said, heading their way. "What trouble are you four up to?"

"None at all," Helen said breezily, watching as Molly gave one last wag of her tail, then headed off toward Luke and Pepper's house, as was her recent custom. "You lost your dog to Toby and Josh, Hiram," she said with a grin.

"I'm okay with that," he said. "She still eats lunch with me every day."

"I'm so glad," Pansy said, "that we went to Union Junction that day and learned about Men Only Day. Ladies Only Day has been so good for this town."

"I still say," Duke said, "that you use that day in your saloon as an excuse to plot against us poor males."

"And do you mind?" Pansy asked with a sweet smile.

"Not at all," Duke said. "Not at all."

* * * * *

Turn the page for a sneak preview of
IF I'D NEVER KNOWN YOUR LOVE
by
Georgia Bockoven

From the brand-new series
Harlequin Everlasting Love
Every great love has a story to tell. ™

One year, five months and four days missing

There's no way for you to know this, Evan, but I haven't written to you for a few months. Actually, it's been almost a year. I had a hard time picking up a pen once more after we paid the second ransom and then received a letter saying it wasn't enough. I was so sure you were coming home that I took the kids along to Bogotá so they could fly home with you and me, something I swore I'd never do. I've fallen in love with Colombia and the people who've opened their hearts to me. But fear is a constant companion when I'm there. I won't ever expose our children to that kind of danger again.

I'm at a loss over what to do anymore, Evan. I've begged and pleaded and thrown temper tantrums with every official I can corner, both here and at home. They've been incredibly tolerant and understanding, but in the end, as ineffectual as the rest of us.

I try to imagine what your life is like now, what you do every day, what you're wearing, what you eat. I want to believe that the people who have you are misguided yet kind, that they treat you well. It's how I survive day to day. To think of you being mistreated hurts too much. If I picture you locked away somewhere and suffering a weight descends on me that makes it almost impossible to get out of bed in the morning.

Your captors surely know you by now. They have to recognize what a good man you are. I imagine you working with their children, telling them that you have children, too, showing them the pictures you carry in your wallet. Can't the men who have you understand how much your children miss you? How can it not matter to them?

How can they keep you away from us all this time? Over and over, we've done what they asked. Are they oblivious to the depth of their cruelty? What kind of people are they that they don't care?

I used to keep a calendar beside our bed next to the peach rose you picked for me before you left. Every night I marked another day, counting how many you'd been gone. I don't do that any longer. I don't want to be reminded of all the days we'll never get back.

When I can't sleep at night, I tell you about my day. I imagine you hearing me and smiling over the details that make up my life now. I never tell you how defeated I feel at moments or how hard I work to hide it from everyone for fear they will see it as a reason to stop believing you are coming home to us.

And I couldn't tell you about the lump I found in my breast and how difficult it was going through all the tests without you here to lean on. The lump was benign—the process of reaching that diagnosis utterly terrifying. I couldn't stop thinking about what would happen to Shelly and Jason if something happened to me.

We need you to come home.

I'm worn down with missing you.

I'm going to read this tomorrow and will probably tear it up or burn it in the fireplace. I don't want you to get the idea I ever doubted what I was doing to free you or thought the work a burden. I would gladly spend the rest of my life at it, even if, in the end, we only had one day together.

You are my life, Evan.

I will love you forever.

* * * * *

Don't miss this deeply moving
Harlequin Everlasting Love story
about a woman's struggle to bring back
her kidnapped husband from Colombia
and her turmoil over whether to let go,
finally, and welcome another man into her life.
IF I'D NEVER KNOWN YOUR LOVE
by Georgia Bockoven
is available March 27, 2007.

And also look for
THE NIGHT WE MET
by Tara Taylor Quinn,
a story about finding love
when you least expect it.

HARLEQUIN® *Romance*®

presents a brand-new trilogy by

PATRICIA THAYER

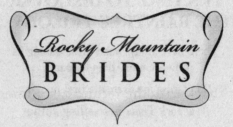

Rocky Mountain
B R I D E S

Three sisters come home to wed.

In April don't miss
Raising the Rancher's Family,

followed by
The Sheriff's Pregnant Wife,
on sale May 2007,

and

A Mother for the Tycoon's Child,
on sale June 2007.

www.eHarlequin.com

HRMAR07

Silhouette®

Romantic
SUSPENSE

Excitement, danger
and passion guaranteed!

USA TODAY bestselling author
Marie Ferrarella
is back with the second installment
in her popular miniseries,
The Doctors Pulaski: Medicine
just got more interesting...
DIAGNOSIS: DANGER is on sale
April 2007 from Silhouette®
Romantic Suspense (formerly
Silhouette Intimate Moments).

Look for it wherever
you buy books!

EVERLASTING LOVE™

Every great love has a story to tell™

Available March 27

And look for
***The Marriage Bed* by Judith Arnold**
and
***Family Stories* by Tessa Mcdermid,**
from Harlequin® Everlasting Love™
this May.

*If you're a romantic at heart, you'll definitely
want to read this new series. Pick up a book today!*

www.eHarlequin.com

HELAPR07

REQUEST YOUR FREE BOOKS!
2 FREE NOVELS PLUS 2
FREE GIFTS!

American | **ROMANCE**®

Heart, Home & Happiness!

YES! Please send me 2 FREE Harlequin American Romance® novels and my 2 FREE gifts. After receiving them, if I don't wish to receive any more books, I can return the shipping statement marked "cancel." If I don't cancel, I will receive 4 brand-new novels every month and be billed just $4.24 per book in the U.S., or $4.99 per book in Canada, plus 25¢ shipping and handling per book and applicable taxes, if any*. That's a savings of close to 15% off the cover price! I understand that accepting the 2 free books and gifts places me under no obligation to buy anything. I can always return a shipment and cancel at any time. Even if I never buy another book from Harlequin, the two free books and gifts are mine to keep forever.

154 HDN EEZK 354 HDN EEZV

Name _____ (PLEASE PRINT)

Address _____ Apt. #

City _____ State/Prov. _____ Zip/Postal Code

Signature (if under 18, a parent or guardian must sign)

Mail to the **Harlequin Reader Service**®:
IN U.S.A.: P.O. Box 1867, Buffalo, NY 14240-1867
IN CANADA: P.O. Box 609, Fort Erie, Ontario L2A 5X3

Not valid to current Harlequin American Romance subscribers.

Want to try two free books from another line?
Call 1-800-873-8635 or visit www.morefreebooks.com.

* Terms and prices subject to change without notice. NY residents add applicable sales tax. Canadian residents will be charged applicable provincial taxes and GST. This offer is limited to one order per household. All orders subject to approval. Credit or debit balances in a customer's account(s) may be offset by any other outstanding balance owed by or to the customer. Please allow 4 to 6 weeks for delivery.

Your Privacy: Harlequin is committed to protecting your privacy. Our Privacy Policy is available online at www.eHarlequin.com or upon request from the Reader Service. From time to time we make our lists of customers available to reputable firms who may have a product or service of interest to you. If you would prefer we not share your name and address, please check here. ☐

HAR07

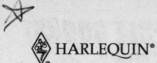

HARLEQUIN®

American ROMANCE®

COMING NEXT MONTH

www.eHarlequin.com

HARCNM0307